John Taylor

A Sketch of Moral Philosophy

An essay to demonstrate the principles of virtue and religion upon a new,

natural, and easy plan

John Taylor

A Sketch of Moral Philosophy
An essay to demonstrate the principles of virtue and religion upon a new, natural, and easy plan

ISBN/EAN: 9783337392369

Printed in Europe, USA, Canada, Australia, Japan

Cover: Foto ©Andreas Hilbeck / pixelio.de

More available books at **www.hansebooks.com**

A

SKETCH

O F

Moral Philofophy ;

OR AN

ESSAY

To demonftrate the Principles of

VIRTUE and RELIGION

UPON

A New, Natural, and Eafy PLAN.

By JOHN TAYLOR, late of NORWICH, D. D.

LONDON:

Printed for J. WAUGH, at the Turk's-head in Lombard-
ftreet; and W. FENNER, at the Angel and Bible in Pater-
nofter-row. M.DCC.LX.

THE

PREFACE.

READER,

THE chief Defign of this Treatife is to eftablifh and explain the Principles relating to the Foundation, or primary Reafon, of Virtue. And therefore, if any Propofitions, or Affertions, which do not immediately relate to them, fhould appear to be dubious, let it be remembered, that the main Scheme may not thereby be affected ; but, for all that, may ftand firm upon it's own Foundation. Thofe Principles are here confidered fimply and abfolutely in themfelves, as the Ground, or Reafon, of right Action, without attending to the Confequences of fuch Action, or what Good may follow from it. Juft as in Euclid, the fimple Principles of Geometry are demonftrated, in a Series of Propofitions, without confidering the Purpofes to

A 2

which

which they may be applied. The Principles are my own, the Result of my own Reflections; and so is the Plan. But I have freely extracted Explications and Improvements out of an excellent Book, intitled, An Enquiry concerning Virtue and Happiness, *published* 1751; *the Work of my worthy, and much esteemed Friend,* Philips Glover *Esq; late of* Wispington *in* Lincolnshire; *with whom I had frequent Conversations upon this Subject for several Years; which, perhaps, may give me some Right to any Thing in that Book that may be useful in this. The same Liberty I have taken with another valuable Performance, which doth much Honor to the Author, and Service to the Cause; I mean the Reverend Mr.* Price's Review, &c. *published last Year.*

This Piece of mine is not a System, *but a* Sketch; *originally designed for young Students, only as an Introduction to the reading of* Woolaston's Religion of Nature delineated, *and now published chiefly for their Use. I wish it may prove a Hint to some abler Hand to bring it to a greater Degree of Perfection.*

Warrington
Septem. 3. 1759.

John Taylor.

A
S K E T C H
O F
MORAL PHILOSOPHY.

The INTRODUCTION.

T O have a clear View, and solid Conviction of the Principles and Obligations of Virtue, or natural Religion, as ftanding upon an eternal and immutable Foundation, muft give great Satisfaction, Affurance and Stability to any Mind in the Practice of all Duty. But it is of fingular Importance to the Study of the facred Writings : not only to prove, in general, the Truth of Revelation ; but alfo to explain the particular Doctrines therein contained. For every Dif-

penfation

penfation and Doctrine, which is of God, muft neceffarily be in Confiftency with what He hath already difcovered to us in the Natures of Things, and the certain Deductions of Reafon from them. This is the principal Clue, which muft guide us in our Searches into Revelation. Revelation is of no Ufe to us, if it is not an Addrefs to the Underftanding and common Senfe of Mankind. And therefore, without a faithful Ufe of our own Faculties, and a proper Acquaintance with the Principles of Truth and Reafon, by miftaking the Senfe and Phrafes of the Scriptures, we may be led to deduce from them fuch Doctrines as are altogether unworthy of God, and the Reproach of Reafon and Humanity. Which, in Fact, hath been the Cafe. But if the Judgment is well fettled in the true Principles of natural Religion, we fhall be furnifhed with a Standard, by which to meafure every Part of Revelation ; a Standard of the fame Authority with Revelation it felf. And it muft be the ftrongeft Confirmation of any Revelation, and give the Student the greateft Satisfaction of the Truth of its Doctrines, when he fees plainly, that they are all worthy of the Wifdom and Goodnefs of God, and perfectly confonant to all the Appearances of Nature, and to the true State of Things in our World. Thus Reafon, rightly directed, will affift and guide Criticifm ; and juft Criticifm

will

will confirm the Dictates of Reason; and
both will join their Forces in fixing the Judgment upon a folid Bafis, and in giving a fatif-
factory and pleafing View of the Principles
of Chriftianity.

When the Principles and Laws of Virtue
are drawn up into an artificial Scheme, it
may look as if they were abftrufe, and required great Depth of Skill to difcover them.
But the contrary is true. The Rule of right
Action lies open to every honeft Mind; and
all Men fee, or may fee, the Difference between moral Good and Evil, as plainly as
they fee with their Eyes the Difference of
Objects which are before them. But though
the Ufe of Sight is familiar to every Body,
yet when it is treated of philofophically,
many Things muft be confidered and ex-
plained by the Rules of Art, which are not
obvious to every Underftanding. Nothing is
more common than the Ufe of Speech : but
to refolve it in it's grammatical Principles,
and to underftand all it's Elegancies, is the
peculiar Advantage only of the learned. In
like Manner, though the Rule of right Action is plane to every Capacity, yet, when we
come to fhew it's Foundation, Obligations
and Extent, and to explane the Faculties of
the Mind, by which it is exerted and applied, we are obliged by the Laws of Art and
Method, to take in many Particulars and

A 4 Argu-

Arguments, which the Bulk of Mankind are not acquainted with. They, if their Hearts are but true, can perform their Duty fufficiently well, without fuch a nice and curious Detail of abftract Reafonings. For as all Virtue is founded in *Truth*, the Rule of Virtue muft be as plane and certain as that Truth, which every Man has a Capacity and Opportunity of underftanding ; beyond which his Obligations cannot extend. Neverthelefs, fuch a methodical and accurate Difquifition is of great Ufe to thofe who have Leifure and Inclination to gain the moft perfect Knowledge of the Principles of Morality.

THE primary Reafon, or Foundation of Virtue, is that Principle, which being fuppofed, Virtue, or Action morally right, neceffarily refults ; which being taken away, there remains no Ground, nor Reafon for Virtue.

WHICH Principle fhould have the following Properties.

1. IT fhould be fo demonftrative as to lay the Mind under the fame Force of Evidence as any demonftrated Propofition in *Euclid*. But obferve ; Demonftration in Morality may be affected by Paffion and Prejudice : and therefore, how ftrong and clear foever it is, may not be feen, or not affented to, through
fome

. some wrong Byafs, or Difpofition of Mind.*
This is a Difadvantage, to which mathematical Demonftration is not fubject. Men cannot fee moral Truth in it's proper Light, unlefs their Minds be well tempered and difpo-
fed. It is neceffary, therefore, that every
Perfon bring to this Study a Mind difengaged
from all partial and irregular Affections, and
quite free and open to the Truth.

2. It fhould be an univerfal Principle, at
all Times, and in all Places, to all moral
Agents invariably the fame. Otherwife, Virtue will be uncertain and precarious.

3. It fhould be perfectly confiftent with
Liberty, or Freedom of Choice. Otherwife
it will, in it's own Nature, be deftructive of
Virtue or Morality; as will afterwards be
fhewn.

THE

* THE famous Mr. *Hobbes* took it into his Head to
fquare the Circle, and to folve many other Problems of
a difficult Nature; but being baffled and confuted in thefe
Attempts, by many learned Men, he, in a kind of Re-
venge, wrote an elaborate Book to difprove the 47th
Prop. of the firft Book of *Euclid*. Now had that Pro-
pofition been oppofite to the Prepoffeffions, Paffions,
Lufts or temporal Interefts of Mankind, doubtlefs Mr.
Hobbes would have had many Followers, notwithftand-
ing the cleareft Demonftration of the Truth of it. See
Harris's Obfervations critical and mifcellaneous. Pref.
P. 6.

THE following Sketch is an Essay towards reprefenting the Foundation of Morality in a Manner agreeable to thofe Properties.

C H A P. I.

Of right and wrong Actions fimply confidered.

D E F I N I T I O N S.

I. *T*HE *Nature of any Thing is all that is contained within the Compafs of it's Being* ; or all that can be truly known, or affirmed of it, namely, all it's Parts, Powers, Properties, Qualities, Relations, Circumftances, whereby it is diftinguifhed from all other Beings of a different Kind, or of different Parts, Powers, Properties, Relations and Circumftances. Or, the Nature of a Thing is it's true Definition, defcribing it to be what it really is. Or, it is an Idea in the Mind, apprehending a Thing to be what it truly is in it felf. So the Nature of a Man, or of any Action, is the fame as the true Definition, or Idea of a Man, or of any Action.

NOTE; When I any where mention the *Natures of Things*, abfolutely, I thereby mean their whole real Being; as in the above Definition. But when I fpeak of the *Natures of Things*, as the Objects of human

Under-

Underftanding, or moral Agency, I mean the Natures of Things as they appear to, or may be known by, our limited Capacities. Which, with regard to Morality, is the fame Thing, as if we underftood them ever fo perfectly.

II. *INTELLIGENCE, or Underftand-ing, is that Faculty, whereby we perceive and compare the Natures of Things.*

III. POSTULATES, or Things taken for granted.

1. THAT there is a GOD, the firft Caufe of all Things, infinite in every natural and moral Perfection.

2. THAT there is a Difference between Perfons, Things, Actions, Relations, Cafes and Circumftances.

PROPOSITIONS.

IV. *Things that are different are treated in a different Manner.* Iron is treated, or ufed, in a different Manner from *Wood, Lead* from *Wool, Fire* from *Water*, &c. This is the primary Law of Action, and, in fact, the Senfe and Practice of all Mankind.

V. *DIF-*

V. *DIFFERENT Things are treated in a different Manner, because their Natures appear to us to differ.* It is of the apparent and experienced Nature of Iron to bear the Violence of Fire, and thereby to be made so soft and ductil, that it may be hammered into various Forms. But we find, that the Nature of Wood, will not bear the Violence of Fire in the same Manner. Therefore, the Carpenter and Smith work Wood and Iron in a different Way, suitably to their different Natures : the Carpenter in the Way, which suits, or fits, Wood ; and the Smith in the Way, which suits Iron.

VI. *TO treat, or use, different Things, agreeably to their apparent different Natures* ; or, *to treat Things according to what we know of their Natures, is to act rightly*, or is right Action. *And to do otherwise, is to act wrong*, or is wrong Action ; as it is acting contrary to what we know of the Natures of Things.

VII. *THUS, the Difference of Actions results naturally from the Difference of Objects.* For if there was no Difference of Things, or Objects, there would be no Reason, or Ground, for any Difference of Actions. No Action could be either right or wrong ; but, all Things being alike, all Actions would be alike ;

alike ; and we might, for any Reafon to the contrary, treat, ufe, or act towards all Things in the fame Manner.

VIII. *T H E Rightnefs of an Action*, or the right Treatment of an Object, *doth not depend upon the Will or Power of him that performs it.* Or, an Action is not therefore right, merely becaufe the Agent chufeth, or hath it in his Power, to act as he pleafeth. But the Rightnefs of the Action confifts in the right Treatment of the *Object*, or in treating the Object according to it's known Nature and Properties. The known Nature and Properties of the *Object* do determine and prefcribe the Rightnefs of the Action. It is in the Power and Choice of the Workman to endeavour to work Wood in the fame Manner as Iron. But it is felf-evident, that his Power and Choice doth not make the Action to be right : becaufe, independent of his Power and Will, the Nature of the Object makes it to be wrong : and, confequently, independent of the Power and Will of any other Being.

IX. *THE Rightnefs of an Action*, or the right Treatment of an Object, *is not affected by good or bad Confequences* ; or by the Good or Harm, which may refult from it. If the Workman treats his Materials according to their true Natures, the Action is right,

[Prop.

[Prop. VI.] whether the Ship happens to be used for Piracy, or fair Trade ; or the Sword for Defence, or Murther.

X. *THE Rightnefs of an Action is not affected by any Lofs or Gain which may accrue to the Author of it.* Lofs or Gain forefeen may affect his Mind by Way of Difcouragement or Motive ; but are effentially diftinct from the Action it felf, and follow it, or are confidered as following it, after it is done, and hath received it's whole true Nature and Properties ; and therefore cannot alter it's Nature, caufe it to be what it is not, or make it to be wrong, when it is in it felf right. For the fame Reafon,

XI. *THE Rightnefs of an Action is not affected by the after Reflections, or Affections of the Author, or of any other Perfon.* Approbation, Applaufe, Satisfaction, Pleafure, *&c.* are all effentially different from the Action, and follow it after it is done, and hath received it's whole true Nature and Properties : and therefore can only fhew what the Author, or others, do think of it, or how they are affected with it ; but cannot conftitute it's Nature, in Whole or in Part, or give it any of it's Qualities. Or, if Approbation, Applaufe, *&c.* are previoufly confidered, they may influence as Motives to the Action ; but cannot affect the Rightnefs of
it

it in it felf; feeing it muft be previoufly fuppofed to be done and finifhed, before they
can be fuppofed to be Motives to it.

XII. *TO right Action, thus confidered,* or
confidered only with refpect to the Nature
and Properties of the Object, *we are not o-
bliged by any private Gain or Advantage; nor
by any Compact or Agreement between Party and
Party; nor by the Will, Command, or Force of
any fuperior Power or Authority; but purely
by the Nature of the Thing,* antecedently to
all pofitive Laws and Sanctions, and independently of all Will and Power whatever.
Which may properly be called a *natural Obligation,* as it is involved in the Natures of
Things, and immediately refulteth only and
wholly from them, fo far as we know
them.*

XIII. De-

---

* To fay, that to treat an Object, or to do a Thing
rightly, according to it's known Nature, is not obligatory *in it felf,* without regard to any private Advantage,
or to any Will or Power, is a manifeft Contradiction.
It is to fay, that a Thing is what it is not; or that we
are not *obliged* to do what, according to the Nature of
the Thing, it is *right* to do. And fuppofe a Perfon
fhould gain by doing a Thing *wrong,* or lofe by doing it
right, ftill the *Right* and *Wrong* of the Action, in it felf
confidered, would be the fame, whatever he gaineth or
lofeth. His Lofs or Gain may affect his Purfe, but doth
not change the Nature of the Action. So the Authority or Power of a Superior may command or force an
Inferior to do what is *wrong;* but that Command or
Force

XIII. DEFINIT. By Obligation, in this Treatife, 1 mean, *A Reafon for acting in any particular Manner, refulting from the Natures of Things, and fhewing that fuch an Action is agreeable to them*; and therefore, that it is reafonable, or fit to be done. Or, *Obligation is the Reafonablenefs of treating Things according to their feveral different Natures.*

XIV. *TO know the Natures of Things, is the fame as to know the Obligation to right Action.*

XV. COROL. 1. *The primary Obligation to right Action is to gain the moft exact Knowledge, we are able, of the Natures of thofe Things, in which we are concerned.* Otherwife we cannot know whether we treat them right or wrong. Therefore,

XVI. COROL. 2. *Our own Underftanding, and the Cultivation of it, is the primary Object of right Action.* Or, he that would act rightly, muft begin with ufing his Underftanding rightly.

XVII. *THE*

Force doth not change the Nature of the Action, or make it to be *right*; becaufe it is in it felf, or in it's own Nature, *wrong*.

XVII. *T H E Obligation to right Action muft be univerfally binding to all intelligent Beings, at all Times, and in all Places.* For where ever, and when ever there hath been, is, or fhall be Difference in the Natures of Things, every intelligent Being, fo far as, in the due Exercife of it's Powers, it fees that Difference, hath been, is, and will be for ever obliged to act agreeably to it. Prop. XIV.

XVIII. FROM the Whole, it follows ; That right Action hath a real Foundation, not in the Profpect of Gain ; nor in the Will, Power, Command, Law or Authority of any Being whatever ; but in the different Natures of Things, as they are perceived by an intelligent Being. And that, the different Natures of Things being fuppofed, Obligation to right Action neceffarily refults ; being taken away, there can be no Reafon or Ground for it.

C H A P. II.

Of Truth.

XIX. *T H E true Natures of Things, and the Truth do coincide, or are the fame.*

B   BECAUSE

BECAUSE *all* the Truth, that can poffibly be conceived, or fpoken of Things, is contained in their Natures, and the Properties, Relations, Circumftances belonging to them. [Prop. I.] Nor is there any *Truth,* that can be known, or declared, concerning them, but what is contained in their Natures, *&c.* Thus the Natures, *&c.* of all Things do comprehend and include all the Truth that can be known in the whole Univerfe. This is *Truth* in the primary and moft proper Senfe.

TRUTH may alfo fignify the Conformity of our Ideas to the real Natures of Things in Oppofition to Error or Fiction. This is the Truth of Ideas, or their Agreement with the Truth of Objects, whether fuch Truth be only conceived in the Mind, or expreffed in Definitions. And this Species of Truth, fo far as it is conformable to the real Natures of Things, or gives true Definitions of them, coincides and comes under the fame Rules with Truth in the primary and moft proper Senfe.

Truth is alfo ufed to fignify the Conformity of our Words to the Apprehenfion or Senfe of our Minds, in Oppofition to Deceit or Lying. But it is *Truth,* in the two preceding Senfes, which we are now explaining, and

and which is principally intended in this Treatife.

XX. *TRUTH, or the true Natures of Things, exifts neceffarily, and therefore eternally, independently, univerfally and unchangeably.*

DEFIN. *Neceffity is either* independent *of all Will and Power univerfally* ; *or* independent *only of fome particular Will and Power* : *it is either* abfolute, *or* relative ; antecedent, *or* confequent. Neceffity *univerfally independent, abfolute* and. *antecedent* is the Neceffity by which GOD exifts ; and is Neceffity in the very Nature of the Thing, as it implies a Contradiction not to exift ; and is not produced by any antecedent Caufe, or Agent, but exifts antecedent to all Caufes and A-gents befides it felf. *Relative* Neceffity, or Neceffity *independent* only on fome particular Will or Power, is Neceffity in fome Refpect only : as when I am impelled, or conftrained, by a fuperior Power to be moved againft my Will. I then am moved by a Neceffity *relative* to my Weaknefs ; becaufe I am not able to refift the fuperior impelling Power. *Confequent* Neceffity is the neceffary Refult of Exiftence, and may be applied to any contingent, or created Being in confequence of it's Exiftence. For when it doth exift, it muft exift neceffarily in this Refpect, that it cannot both exift, and not exift, at the

fame

fame Time. And by the fame Neceffity, it muft neceffarily exift in the *Manner* in which it doth exift. That is to fay, with the Nature, Properties, Qualities with which, and in the Relations and Circumftances, in which, it doth exift. So that, though the great GOD may create Beings with what various Natures, Properties, &c. he pleafeth ; yet there is a Neceffity, a *confequent* Neceffity, that every Thing, when he hath created it, fhould exift, with the Nature and Properties, and in the feveral Relations and Circumftances, in which he hath made it to exift. And as the Nature, Properties, Relations and Circumftances of every Being do include the whole Truth, or all the Truths which can belong to that Being, or be truly affirmed of it [by Prop. XIX.] therefore I fay, that the Truths belonging to fuch a Being are *confequentially* neceffary, or neceffarily refult from it's Nature, and cannot but be contained in it. Nor is it in the Power of any Being whatever to make it true, that thofe Truths do not belong to it's Nature, while that Nature continues the fame. For Inftance ; it is in the Will and Pleafure of GOD, whether he will, or will not, create two fuch Beings as a MAN and a HORSE, under their particular Natures, Properties, Relations and Circumftances. But when he has made a MAN, that Being muft of Neceffity be a MAN, endowed with the Nature

ture and Properties of a Man, and in the particular Relations and Circumstances in which he is produced and placed. And so, when God has made an Horse, or any other Creature, all the Truths included in it's Nature, Properties, &c. or it's real Idea, muft exift. For, though no created Being exifteth neceffarily, yet every Being, when created, is neceffarily what it is.

And, to advance a Step further; as the Nature, *i. e.* the real Idea, or Definition of a *Man*, or of any other particular Being, always was, and always will be, what it now is; juft as much as the Nature of a *Triangle*, with all it's Properties and Proportions, always was, and always will be, what it now is, whether a Man, or Triangle ever *actually* exifted or not, (as fuch Ideas do not depend upon any Fact, or real Exiftence of Things,) therefore I fay, that fuch Ideas or Truths belonging to the Natures of a Man, Horfe, Triangle, are *abfolutely neceffary*; and confequently, *independent, eternal, univerfal, immutable*, always and every where the fame. For whatever exifts by *abfolute Neceffity*, can be affected by no Will or Power, by no Time or Place; but muft be independent, eternal, univerfal and unchangeable. Infinite Power, may turn a *Man* into a *Horfe*, or a *Horfe* into a *Man*; a *Triangle* into a *Circle*, or a *Circle* into a *Triangle*. But

no

no Power, in any Part of the Univerſe, from all Eternity even to all Eternity, could, or can ever change or turn the Idea, or Truths belonging to a *Man*, or to a *Triangle* into the Idea, or Truths belonging to a *Horſe*, or a *Circle*. Theſe muſt remain for ever and immutably the ſame. For though *Beings* are mutable, as to their *actual* Natures, yet the *Truths* belonging to their Natures, (or their *ideal* Natures,) are not mutable. Seeing the Idea, or Definition of a *Horſe*, as ſuch, can never become the Idea, or Definition of a *Man*, as ſuch, or of any other Thing or Being. Thus Truth, even all Truth, which relates to all actual and poſſible Beings, ex-iſts by an *antecedent*, or *abſolute* Neceſſity. For as it is true, that there never was a Time when, nor Place where, the great GOD was any other than what he is now ; ſo it is true, that there never was a Time when, nor Place where, the Idea of a Triangle or a Man was any other than what it is now.

IT is alſo true, That the *Relations*, or Reſ-pect, which Things bear to one another, are, in their Natures, or Ideas, in the ſame Manner, neceſſary, eternal, and unalterable. For the Idea of a *Creator*, always did, and always neceſſarily muſt have reſpect to the Idea of a *Creature* ; and *vice verſâ*. The Idea of a *Father* always was, and muſt ne-ceſſarily be always, connected with the Idea

of

of a *Son* or *Daughter :* and *vice verſâ.*——
Circumſtances are only the *Relations* of a Being to it's Situation, to the Things that are
about it, or to the Objects of it's Perception.
——*Proportion* too is but the *Relations* of
higher or lower, ſtronger or weaker, more
or leſs, as to Degrees of Being, Powers,
Senſes, Capacities, or Faculties : and therefore, both theſe muſt come under the ſame
Rule with *Relations* in general.

XXI. Corol. Hence it follows ; that the
Natures, *i. e.* the Ideas or Definitions, and
Relations of all Things whatſoever, or the
Truths belonging to them, are as neceſſary,
independent, univerſal and immutable, as
the Ideas, Definitions and Relations, or Proportions of Lines and Figures in Geometry.
For if there is a real Difference between the
true Nature, or the true Definition or Idea,
of a Man, and of a Horſe, or of any other
Thing, that Difference was always, and always will be the ſame. Becauſe the Idea,
or true Definition of a Man, and of a Horſe,
or of any other Thing, or the Truths belonging to them, never could, nor ever can
be any other than what they are now, at
this Time. Therefore, their Difference, together with the Properties, Relations, Proportions, Circumſtances, which neceſſarily
attend, or reſult from that Difference, muſt
always be the ſame, as really and truly as

the Difference, and different Properties, Relations and Proportions of a Circle and Triangle, or any other geometrical Figure.

XXII. *ALL the Obligations that result, or flow from, the Truth, or the true Natures of Things, are necessary, and therefore independent, eternal, universal, and immutable.*

THAT Obligation to right Action immediately results from the Truth, or the true Natures, &c. of Things, hath been established by Prop. VII, XII. And that the Truth, or the true Natures of Things, do exist *necessarily*, &c. hath been proved under the preceding Proposition. Hence it follows; That whatever immediately results from a *necessary* Existence, as such, must result *necessarily*, or be *necessary*. But Obligation to right Action immediately results, or follows from a *necessary* Existence, as such, namely, the Truth, &c. therefore, such Obligation must result *necessarily*, or be *necessary*. It results necessarily, because it is no other than the necessary Existence of it self, or the true Idea of it, considered as what it is, with Respect to the Usage or Treatment of the Object to which it belongs. Prop. XIV. And therefore, because it is what it is, and the Idea of it cannot be changed, we are, *by the Nature of the Thing*, necessarily obliged to use and treat the Object according to
what

what it is. Not, that an Obligation of *Con-straint* is laid upon the Mind in Fact, or actually, to treat it according to what it is, fo, as that the Mind cannot poffibly do otherwife. The Mind of an intelligent Being may be fuppofed to act in what Manner it pleafeth. But it is an Obligation of *right Direction*, or of a true, infallible Rule, that is laid before the Mind ; which Rule is the Nature of the Thing, or the Truth belonging to it, neceffarily requiring, that it be treated according to that Nature, or Truth, and not otherwife : and demonftrating, that if is treated in a Manner different from it's Nature, it is treated wrong. [Prop. VI.] The Nature of the Thing ftands before the Mind as neceffary, or as what it is. And in that neceffary Nature the Obligation lies ; and therefore neceffarily rifes or refults from it, as it determines and fhews the only true and right Manner in which it is to be treated, whether the Mind attends to it, or not ; or treats it agreeably to it's Nature, or not. From the Idea or Nature of Man an Obligation neceffarily refults, or ftands before the Mind, to confider and treat him as what he is, or as a Man ; and fhews, that there is no other Way of treating him rightly. From the Idea or Nature of a Triangle arifes an Obligation to confider and apply it in Mathematics, or in Works of Art, according to it's true Nature : otherwife, it will be

wrong

wrong confidered, or applied, by the fame
Propofition. And this Obligation is univerfal and eternal, by Prop. XVII. Nor doth
it depend upon any Gain or Advantage, upon any Compact or Agreement ; upon any
Will, Command or Force of any fuperior
Power or Authority ; but is neceffary and
independent. [Prop. XII.]

XXIII. Corol. I. *The Obligations of
Truth do not depend upon the arbitrary Will
of GOD.* Prop. XII.

XXIV. Corol. II. *The great GOD himfelf is neceffarily under the Obligations of
Truth.*

God is neceffarily what he is, as to his *actual* as well as *ideal* Exiftence, and he neceffarily knows this. And he as neceffarily
knows all the Natures, Capacities, Relations
and Circumftances of all Things, which he
hath produced, becaufe he hath produced
them. Nor can he poffibly conceive, or
confider them to be any other, or in any
Refpect otherwife, than what, and as what
he has made them. And therefore, the
fame Obligations muft neceffarily refult from
their Natures, Capacities, &c. to treat them,
or to deal with them, according to their ref-
pective Natures, &c. as refult to any other intelligent Being. For if thofe Obligations refult

fult *neceffarily*, [Prop. XXII.] they muft refult *univerfally*, to one intelligent Nature as well as to another. For though the Extent or Degree of the Knowledge of the Natures, *&c.* of the Beings that exift, muft be according to the Extent or Degree of Intelligence, with which any Being is endowed ; yet the refulting of thofe Obligations neceffarily from the Natures of Things hath no Connection with, nor Dependence upon, any Perception or Knowledge of any Being whatever : but is connected with, and depends upon, *only* the Natures, *&c.* from which fuch Obligations refult. And therefore, thofe Obligations muft refult equally to all Minds that confider, or are acquainted with them ; as their Exiftence neither is, nor can be affected (altered or changed) by any Mind, that confiders and obferves them, feeing they have no Dependence on any Mind whatfoever ; but refult neceffarily from the Natures of Things. The great GOD may create what Beings he thinks fit. But when he hath created any Beings, the Natures, *&c.* of thofe Beings muft be what they are, independently even of his Will, and only with Refpect to their own Exiftence and Situation, what and where they are. And as He, who made all Things, muft have the moft perfect and extenfive Knowledge of all Natures, *&c.* and can never have any poffible Reafon, or Inducement, to act contrary to them, it is infallibly certain,

that

that he always will actually treat and deal
with them according to their true Natures,
Properties, Relations or Circumſtances ; or
according to what they really are : unleſs he
will contradict, or act inconſiſtently with, his
own certain Knowledge, or violate a known
Obligation, and ſo be ſelf-condemned ; which
is abſurd. Therefore, the Divine Being,
though he hath no Superior to direct him,
and though his Happineſs can neither be in-
creaſed, nor diminiſhed, muſt be as neceſſarily
obliged to obſerve Truth and Reaſon in all
his Actions, as any other intelligent Nature :
and that, as much more perfectly and ſtrong-
ly, as he doth more perfectly perceive thoſe
eternal and neceſſary Obligations. And his
Divine Rectitude, or Perfection of Holineſs,
conſiſts in his conſtant and invariable Conformity to this eternal and immutable Rule
of all right Action. Which indeed is no o-
ther than his own infinite, eternal and all-
perfect Underſtanding ; which Underſtanding is the eternal and unchangeable Law, or
Rule by which He is directed in all his Actions.

FROM theſe Propoſitions we may deduce the following Axioms, Canons or
Laws of Truth.

XXV. CANON I. [That which is, is] *is
the univerſal Rule of all Truth : as on the
contrary,*

contrary, [that is, which is not ;] *or* [that is not, which is,] *are the univerſal Rules of all Error.* That is to ſay, all Truth and Error may be reduced to thoſe Rules.

XXVI. CANON 2. *All Truth exiſts inde⸗ pendently of all Will and Power whatſoever.* Prop. XX.

XXVII. CANON 3. *No Truth, though of the leaſt Importance, can ever be changed or deſtroyed.* All created Beings may be changed or deſtroyed ; but the Truths belonging to their ſeveral Natures can never, by any Power whatever, be deſtroyed or changed. [Prop. XX.] For as the leaſt Drop of Water, or the ſmalleſt Atom of Duſt, muſt neceſſarily, while it continues in Being, fill up ſome Space, and Mountains heaped upon Mountains cannot cruſh it into Nothing : ſo the leaſt Truth is of Force to refiſt the united Power of the whole Univerſe ; nor can the joint Endeavours of all Beings make it not to be true. Hence, whatever Action we commit at any Time, it muſt be eternally true, that we have done that Action. It is as true now, that the Wickedneſs committed 4000 Years ago, was then committed, as it was the very Day it was done; and muſt remain equally true to all Eternity. Truth may be denied, or forgotten ; but can never be deſtroyed.

XXVIII.

XXVIII. C̲anon 4. *Truth,* as it can never be changed or deſtroyed, *may equally operate in the Mind that is conſcious to it, with the ſame unvaried Force, and have equal Effects upon ſuch a Mind, to all Eternity.*

XXIX. C̲anon 5. *No one Truth can poſſibly be inconſiſtent with any other Truth.* If one Thing be true, it may indeed follow, that another is falſe : but if one Thing be true, it can never follow, that another true Thing is falſe ; becauſe the one is as true as the other, both being founded in the real Nature or Exiſtence of Things.

XXX. C̲anon 6. *Whatever is inconſiſtent with, or contradictory to, Truth, is Falſhood or Error.*

XXXI. C̲anon 7. *A Thing cannot be true and falſe, at the ſame Time, and in the ſame Reſpect.*

XXXII. C̲anon 8. *There are no Degrees of Truth, ſimply conſidered ;* all Truth being equally true, though not equally important. The Truths belonging to the Deity are infinitely more important than the Truths belonging to any Portion of mere Matter. Nevertheleſs, the Truths belonging to both are equally true.

XXXIII.

XXXIII. CANON 9. *There is no Medium between Truth and Falſhood*; as there is no Medium between Exiſtence and Non-Exiſtence.

XXXIV. CANON 10. *No one Intelligence can underſtand that to be true, without Error, which another Intelligence underſtands to be falſe, without Error.* Or, *All Truth muſt be underſtood to be Truth by all intelligent Beings, ſo far as they do underſtand it.*

XXXV. CANON 11. *All Underſtanding muſt neceſſarily be ſubject to Truth.* Or, the true Natures and Exiſtences of Things are the Rule and Meaſure of all Underſtanding, from which no Underſtanding can deviate without falling into Error, or Ignorance. And, underſtanding any Thing to be true, it is not in the Power of any intelligent Being to underſtand it to be falſe, or otherwiſe than as true.

XXXVI. CANON 12. *No Truth whatſoever can be ſubject to any Underſtanding, or Authority whatſoever.* Or, *It is not in the Power of any Underſtanding or Authority to make what it pleaſes to be true.* Truth cannot be determined, decreed, or eſtabliſhed by the Pleaſure, Numbers, or Authority of any Men, or of any other Beings: but is determined

termined and eftablifhed by it's own neceffary Exiftence alone.

XXXVII. Canon 13. *As the great GOD perfectly underftands all Manner of Exiftences, both actual and poffible, his Underftanding muft be a Rule and Meafure of Truth, no lefs perfect than the real Natures of Things, to which it is fully commenfurate.*

C H A P. III.

Of Reason.

XXXVIII. Defin. REASON *is that Faculty of the Mind, by which we perceive, or underftand the Truth, or the true Natures of Things, and are capable of confidering, diftinguifhing, comparing and judging of their Natures, Properties, Circumftances and Relations, and of difcovering what is agreeable to, or inconfiftent with them.* Thus *Reafon* is diftinguifhed from the fimple Perceptions of *Senfe*, or the Feelings of mere animal Nature, fuch as Seeing, Hearing, Smelling, Tafting. Which indeed may generally perceive, or feel, Objects truly; but cannot perceive or apprehend the Truth, or reflect upon their own Feelings, fo as to deduce any Truths from the Natures, or Relations of Objects; which is the Work, not

of

of *Senfe*, but of *Reafon* alone. *Senfe* only
fees a Part, and a Whole : *Reafon* compares
them, and difcovers, that the Whole is e-
qual to all it's Parts. *Senfe* only hears
Sounds : *Reafon* diftinguifhes, compares and
compounds them. Thus *Reafon* is alfo diftinguifhed from *Inflincts* ; which, according
to their true Nature, are to be confidered as
the mechanical Part of our Conftitution ;
feeing they have the fame Effect upon the
Motions of an Animal, as Weights and
Springs upon a Machine, as a Clock, *&c.*
moving, impelling, exciting or determining
the Animal involuntarily, or without
Thought or Reflection. Some Animals feem
to be wholly under the Influence of fuch
mechanical Powers, or Impreffions. However fuch Inftincts we certainly experience in
the Inclinations, Paffions, Affections, Defires and Appetites, which were originally
implanted in our Conftitution, and which are
perpetually working in it : fuch as Fear,
Anger, Love, Hatred, Pity, Affection to
Offspring, an Inclination to Society, Bene-
volence or good Nature, Hunger, Thirft,
&c. Thefe Inftincts are, in themfelves,
manifeftly the inferior Part of our Conftitution, and have no Connection with Reafon,
or Underftanding ; faving only fo far as they
are rightly directed, or governed by it.

C

NOTE ;

Note ; In this Definition of Reason I include both the Faculty, and the Application of it ; the Capacity of perceiving, and the actual Perception of Truth. I also use Reason and Understanding as synonymous.

XXXIX. *REASON is that Principle, in all Beings endowed with it, which is in it's own Nature supreme and commanding* ; before which all Means and Ends, that any Mind is capable of regarding, are to be tried as reasonable or unreasonable ; and accordingly to be pursued or avoided. In Deity, Understanding or Reason is the Principle, which makes all his natural Attributes to be Perfections. For, without Reason, his Being would be reduced to the State of thoughtless Matter, or to an infinite Absurdity. His Immensity would be but as mere Extension, and his Power a boundless Force without Direction. And, without Understanding and Reason, his moral Perfections could have no Existence at all. For it is manifest, that a Being without Reason is altogether uncapable of Justice, Goodness, Truth or Holiness ; or of so much as knowing what they are, or what the proper Objects, upon which they are to be exercised. In short, without Reason, the Divine Nature would be a kind of universal Darkness, and whatever he is necessarily, would be necessarily uncapable of
being

being applied to any proper End. And in human Life, Reason is moſt evidently the reigning Principle, which alone is capable of ordering and directing all Affairs. And in our Conſtitution, it is ſuperior to, and capable of controuling and regulating, all our Paſſions, Affections and Appetites.

XL. *REASON in any Being neceſſarily implies an Obligation upon that Being to right Action.* For Obligation to right Action ariſes neceſſarily from the Natures and Relations of Things, ſo far as they are known, by Prop. XII, XIV. Therefore, where there is the moſt perfect Knowledge of the Natures and Relations of all Beings, as in the moſt high GOD, there the moſt perfect and ſtrongeſt Obligations muſt neceſſarily reſult. And with Regard to all other Beings, the nearer they approach, in the Scale of Being, to the Perfection of Reaſon, the more perfect and extenſive their Obligations to right Action muſt be. And the loweſt Claſs of rational Nature, ſo far as it is capable of knowing the Truth, muſt ſo far neceſſarily be under an Obligation to follow it.

XLI. *WHEN we anſwer this Obligation, and act agreeably to the Truth, or the true Natures, Properties, Relations and Circumſtances of Things, we then act* REASONABLY; or our Actions and Purſuits are
reaſonable.

reafonable. Reafon difcovers, or perceives the Truth ; and we act reafonably, in any Refpect, when we act agreeably to what Reafon difcovers concerning the Natures, Properties, Relations, and Circumftances of Things.

XLII. *THE Faculty of Reafon may be more or lefs perfect in different Beings.* The Difference of mental Capacities is certain. In God, Reafon muft neceffarily be in the higheft Degree of Perfection. In all other Beings, it is in that Degree and Extent, which He is pleafed to allot. And among Men we find, that he has allotted very different Capacities to different Perfons.

XLIII. *BUT Underftanding or Reafon in different Beings, is not different with Refpect to what it truly underftands ; but only in Degree or Extent of Capacity,* by Prop. XXXIV. For Inftance ; fuppofe any rational Being can only underftand the Relation between two and four, or that four is double to two ; though it fhould underftand no other Relation or Proportion ; yet it underftands this, as truly as that Being, whofe rational Capacity is of a higher Degree, or much larger Extent. And thus it's Underftanding is inferior, only as it is lefs extenfive, not as it underftands differently, what it doth underftand, from a fuperior Capacity.

XLIV.

XLIV. *THE Obligations of rational Beings to right Action muſt be according to their ſeveral Degrees of Reaſon, and the Extent of their intellectual Capacities.* For it is very evident, that as no Being can act, ſo no Being can be obliged to act, beyond the Limits of it's natural Powers.

C H A P. IV.

Of Agency.

XLV. Defin. *AGENCY is Liberty of* Mind *to prefer one Thing before another, to will or nill, to chooſe to exert to any Power, or not to exert it.* He who hath a Capacity of chooſing to riſe up, or to ſit ſtill; to ſpeak, or to be ſilent; to turn his Thoughts to this, or to the other Object, is indued with Agency.

XLVI. Freedom *and* Agency *are the ſame Thing.* He that hath Freedom of Mind to chooſe and will, to nill or refuſe, is an Agent. But he that hath not that Freedom is no Agent. To *will* and to *act* are the ſame Thing : and to aſk, if a Man be free, is the ſame as to aſk, if he be an Agent.

XLVII. *THE Exiſtence of any Being, ſeparate and diſtinct from the firſt neceſſarily*

C 3   *exiſting*

exifting Caufe, is fufficient Evidence of the A-gency of the firft Caufe, or fupreme Being. For if any other Being doth exift, it muft either exift neceffarily, or by the Will, or Agency, of the firft Caufe. There is no third Reafon or Ground of Exiftence. It is abfurd, or rather impoffible, that I fhould think myfelf a neceffarily exifting Being, or any Part of fuch a Being : becaufe I know certainly that I have not the Attributes, which neceffarily belong to fuch a Being : I muft therefore either be produced by the Will, or Agency, of fuch a Being, or be neceffarily produced. If the latter, then I exift neceffarily ; feeing that which is necef-farily produced, muft exift by the fame Ne-ceffity, by which it's Caufe doth exift, and muft have the Attributes of a neceffarily exifting Being. But I am fure I have not thofe Attributes : therefore, I am the free Production of the firft Caufe, who had it in his Option to give me Exiftence or not. This fhews, that Agency, or Freedom of Choice, is not impoffible, or a Contradic-tion ; feeing the whole Creation proves, that God, who produced it, produced it vo-luntarily ; and confequently is an *Agent.*

XLVIII. *Man is an Agent.* If Man was free, he could not have greater Confciouf-nefs, or Evidence, of his Freedom than he hath. Any one Inftance of Self-Motion in

us

us will prove us to be Agents. And any
one may give himself at any Time a Demonftration of this, by only ftirring his
Finger, or fhutting his Eyes whenever he
pleafeth. It is unreafonable and abfurd to
fuppofe, that GOD hath given us Underftanding and Judgment without a Power of
ufing them. Or that we fhould be capable
of knowing and reafoning about right Action, and yet not be capable of acting. Our
being neceffarily juftified, or condemned by
the Reflections of our Minds upon our own
Actions, proves that *we* are accountable for
them, as being the proper and only Authors
of them ; and, confequently, that we are
Agents.

XLIX. *AGENCY, or Freedom of Mind,
is the fame in nilling as in willing ; in refufing, as in confenting ; or in choofing not to do
a Thing, as in choofing to do it.* If at prefent
I do not like to do a Thing, and fo refufe to
do it ; but afterwards alter my Mind, and
then am willing to do it, or choofe it fhould
be done : the Freedom of the Mind is e-
qually exerted in refufing to do the Thing,
in altering my Mind, and in choofing to do it.

L. AGENCY, *or a Capacity of willing or
choofing that any Effect fhould be produced,*
and Power, *or an Ability to produce that Effect, are different Things, and may exift the*
C 4   *one*

one without the other. The Power of God is infinite, and perfectly commenfurate to his Agency : infomuch that whatever he wills, is immediately effected. But human Power is confined to very narrow Bounds, and capable of producing, comparatively, but very few Effects : fo that it is eafy to conceive, that we may will, or choofe, to have that done, which is not in our *Power* to effect ; or, that we may will to reft, or not to move, even when a fuperior Power conftrains us to be moved. Further ; any Action is juftly attributed to the Agent, who willed it to be effected, though the Effect did not follow, through Defect of his Power ; or though the Power of another Agent effected it, in Confequence of his willing it. He is a Murderer, who wills the Murther, though he employs a Ruffian to perpetrate what he willeth. Power may poffibly refide in a Subject that is no Agent : as in the Cafe of phyfical or natural Powers ; fuch as Springs, Weights, or the Power of a Body in Motion to impel or move another Body. And Agency may poffibly be in a Subject that hath no Power to produce the external Effect ; as in a Man who hath no Ufe of his Limbs, and yet wills, or defires to walk. For it is very plain ; that Agency, which is the voluntary Exertion of the *Mind*, is not deftroyed by any Obftruction of the Effect. Therefore,

LI. *WANT*

LI. *WANT of Power doth not deftroy Agency.* Indeed, the Confcioufnefs that I want Power to effect a Thing, may prevent my willing of it ; but takes not away my Agency, or Capacity of willing it. And my not acting, or willing, in fuch a Cafe, only fhews my Prudence, not Want of Agency. Though the Body be bound in Fetters, or confined to the clofeft Prifon, the Mind is ftill free, and can, notwithftanding, exert it felf voluntarily. And fo in all Cafes where the Power of effecting, or moving, is want-ing, or is obftructed by a fuperior Power.

LII. *THE Decifion of the* Judgment *for or againft a Thing doth not affect or deftroy, Freedom, or Agency.* The Judgment fimply fhews, what is, or appears to be, right and wrong; and though Men fhould generally be determined to act according to it's Deci-fion ; yet it is certain, from undoubted *Ex-perience* and Facts, which in this Cafe are as good Evidence, as *Experiments* in natural Philofophy, that they are not determined ne-ceffarily, but freely. Not *neceffarily,* by a *relative, particular* Neceffity ; [See the De-finition under Prop. XX.] for then they muft *always* follow the Decifion of the Judgment by the Conftraint of a Force which they are not able to refift. Which is contrary to Ex-perience and Fact. Men too frequently choofe
to

to act contrary to the Decifion of the Judgment concerning Right and Wrong. They fee and acknowledge the Right, and do the Wrong. Otherwife, Men would always, and univerfally do what is morally right, as they would always follow the Dictates of their Judgments ; as will be feen afterwards.

LIII. *FOR the fame Reafon, Motives of Pleafure, or Pain, Profit, or Lofs, do not affect Agency.* Thefe work powerfully upon the human Mind, but not *neceffarily* ; feeing there are many who choofe to act contrary to their Influence. They are abftract Notions, or Confiderations, in the Mind, which therefore, may induce, or incline, but have no Power to compel or force. They are not *Agents*, or *efficient Caufes*, but an *End* propofed, or in View : and therefore, can influence the Mind only as Objects or Ends propofed to it's Confideration. The Profpect or Confideration, of fome very great Evil, Pain or Suffering, which makes it, as we fay, *morally* certain, that I fhall not choofe to do what would bring upon me the dreaded Evil, doth not fufpend, much lefs deftroy, my Freedom, or Agency. In fuch Cafes, my not choofing, or refufing, fhews only my Care or Caution to preferve my Life, Eafe or Safety : or my Fear of Pain and Death ; but not my Want of Liberty. For though it be certain, that I fhall not choofe to do what would bring upon me the

fuppofed

suppofed Evil, yet am I ftill at Liberty to choofe it, did I not prefer the Prefervation of my Life and Safety. My Freedom of Judgment and Choice remains entire : for if I judged it proper, or had Reafons, which determined me to choofe or prefer the contrary, I fhould, at that very Inftant, choofe the contrary. No Man would choofe to have his Flefh burnt with a hot Iron without any Reafon, or when he hath a very good Reafon againft it : but when there is a good Reafon for it, to preferve Life or Limb, he will choofe that the Surgeon fhould apply a Cautery, or hot Iron, to his Flefh. No Man would choofe to be burnt alive : but rather than do Violence to Religion or Confcience, many have gone to the Stake with furprizing Courage and Firmnefs of Mind. No Man would willingly incur the Danger of lofing his Life : but in his Country's Caufe, and for other Reafons, which have appeared to him very important, good and juft, many a Man hath voluntarily expofed his Life to this Danger. We choofe Evil, when of two Evils we choofe the leaft. This plainly proves, that in fuch Cafes a Man choofeth or refufeth, nilleth or willeth, not becaufe his Liberty is affected ; but becaufe he hath, or hath not, Reafons or Motives to determine him this or the other Way. His Agency is the fame both in refufing and in choofing, by Prop. XLIX.

LIV. *AGEN-*

LIV. *AGENCY,* or *Freedom,* admits
not of *Degrees* ; or *cannot be more or lefs,
partly free, and partly forced.* For though
a Being may both act, and be acted upon ;
yet this cannot be in the fame Refpects. For
fo far as any Being acteth, he is perfectly
free : fo far as he is acted upon, he is no A-
gent at all. For,

LV. *A N irrefiftible Impulfe upon the Mind
from fome fuperior Power, which forces us to
will, or to confent, deftroys Agency : or rather
is a Contradiction.* It is impoffible, that the
Will, or free Choice, fhould be forced. And
if it be forced, it cannot, for that Reafon,
be free. For Force neceffarily makes the
Thing, fuppofed to be freely willed, not to
be at all willed, or chofen, by the Being,
who is under the Conftraint of fuch Force.
Therefore, in the Nature of the Thing, the
Will cannot be fubject to any overbearing
Violence. For by fuch Violence it muft
ceafe to be a Will, or an Agent ; and becomes as paffive as inert Matter, when it is
put into Motion by mere Power. Nor can
any Thing, effected in the Mind by mere
Force, be accounted the Action of the Being, in whom it is effected, any more
than the Motion of any Body can be accounted the Action, or freely chofen Motion,
of that Body.

LVI. *THE*

LVI. *THE proper Caufe of an Action is the Will of the Agent, and nothing elfe.* If any Effect is produced by any external *Force* impreffed upon my Mind or Body, that Effect is not my Action, but the Action of that Being, who willed, or chofe, to force me, not indeed to *act*, but to be *moved* in fuch a Manner as to produce the fuppofed Effect : for which I can in no Senfe be accountable, as I was only a paffive Inftrument in the Hand of a fuperior Agent. That Effect being truly and only my Action, which I freely will to exift. Therefore, .

LVII. *ONLY what an Agent* intends *to do is to be accounted his Action.* What arifes beyond or contrary to his Intention, however it may eventually happen, or be derived by the Connection of natural Caufes, from his Determination, ought not to be imputed to him. Our own Determinations alone are our Actions. [LV. LVI.] Thefe alone we have abfolute Power over, and are immediately and truly the Caufes of, and refponfible for. [*Price.*] A Perfon intending to fell a Tree, may accidentally, by the Head's flying from the Helve of the Ax, kill a Man : but this, not being his Intention, is not his Action.

CHAP.

C H A P. V.

Of Virtue, or Action morally right.

LVIII. MORAL Action *comprehends all Instances of Regard or Behaviour towards our selves, and all other rational, and sensible, or mere animal Beings, from the most high GOD down to the meanest Reptil, to which we are related, with which we have any Society, or Intercourse, or which we can any Ways voluntarily affect by our Actions.* These are the Limits of Morality, with Regard to Objects and Actions. Therefore,

LIX. *FROM the Objects and Ideas of Morality we exclude all Things merely material or inanimate, with their Natures and Properties, as Wood, Stone, Iron, Water, Air, &c. and any mechanical Operations, or Actions upon, or relating to them; such as Painting, Sculpture, Building, Musick, &c. excepting only so far as such inanimate Things, or such Operations have any Connection with our Regards to, or Treatment of rational or sensible Beings.* Such Operations may be *simply* right or wrong according to the Natures, or Properties of the Things : that is to say, may be painted, carved, performed, *&c.* truly or agreeably to the true Nature of Things ; but they are
not

not *morally* right or wrong, any further than they are, or are not, done *honeftly, ufefully* or *beneficently.*

LX. *WE muft alfo exclude from the Idea of Morality all mere Knowledge, or Science* ; as Mathematics, Hiftory, Skill in Languages, *&c. As alfo all Ingenuity, cr Sagacity of Mind, Strength, or Agility of Body.* All thefe may, in fome Refpects, bear a Conformity to Truth, or to the true Natures of Things. But being only fimple Knowledge, or Powers, they cannot be *morally* right or wrong, any further than as they are applied ; or are, or are not ufed *honeftly, ufefully,* or *beneficently.* Any Skill, Capacity, Ingenuity or Sagacity in Arts and Sciences may exift, and act with great Truth and Accuracy in Refpect to their particular Objects and Ends, without connoting or influencing right Behaviour, or any good Difpofition of Mind ; and are confiftent with the moft vicious and immoral Lives.

LXI. *AND we may exclude from the Idea of Morality the Performance of any Functions merely natural or animal* ; as eating, drinking, fleeping, *&c.* excepting fo far as Reafon, or Behaviour, are concerned in the Performance of them. For though the performing fuch Functions may be acting according to the true Natures of Things, yet
in

in themfelves they are mere *natural* Actions,
to which, in Part at leaft, we are compelled
by Neceffity of Nature. And fo far they
cannot be judged Actions at all. [XLV,
XLVI.]

LXII. *A L S O all inftinctive Inclinations,
Paffions and Affections, fuch as Fear, Sorrow,
Joy, Compaffion, Love, &c. muft be excluded
from the Notion and Principle of moral Action.*
Seeing thefe are, as it were, the Mechanifm
of our Frame, which move, impel, excite
or determine the animal Part of our Conftitution involuntarily, or without Thought or
Reflection ; and fo far their Motions are no
Actions at all ; nor, while we are under their
Impulfe alone, are we Agents, by Prop.
XLV, XLVI. Confequently, Inftincts can
conftitute no Part or Principle of Morality,
any further than they are overruled, reftrain-
ed, directed and applied by the Interpofition
of Reafon to moral Purpofes.

LXIII. As all the foregoing Rules and
Laws of *right Action fimply confidered,* of
Truth, of *Reafon* and of *Agency,* are univerfally true ; fo they muft neceffarily be true of
Action morally right in particular : and we
have, accordingly, a Right to argue from
them ; or to refer to them, as Truths already eftablifhed.

LXIV. *IF*

LXIV. *IF there was no Difference in the Natures, Relations, and Properties of Persons, Things and Actions ; but all Persons, Things and Actions, and their several Natures, Relations and Properties were the same, in all Respects equal and alike, then there could be no Reason, nor Foundation, for moral Action,* by Prop. VII. Because it muſt then be perfectly indifferent how we behave ; nor could we be under any Obligation to act in this, or in the other Manner ; ſeeing there would be nothing in any *Object,* which required any Difference in our Actions, or Behaviour, all Objects being in all Reſpects the ſame ; a Man, a Horſe, a Tree, a Stone, Money in the Purſe, or Pebbles on the Sea-ſhore ; Blood in the Veins, or Sludge in a Gutter. Nor would there be any Thing in any *Action,* which could make any Difference between it, and it's Oppoſite. Love, Hatred ; Gratitude, Ingratitude ; Intemperance, Sobriety ; Lewdneſs, Chaſtity ; ſtabbing a Man, and running a Spade into a Heap of Clay, would be Actions and Habits all alike, and all alike indifferent, neither morally right, nor morally wrong.

LXV. *BUT there is a real Difference in the Natures, Properties and Relations of Perſons, Things and Actions, which, in ſome Meaſure, is obvious to all Mankind, and*

D   *known*

known and allowed over all the World. Prop.
IV. V.   And this Difference in the Natures,
&c. of Perſons, Things and Actions, (being
in it ſelf neceſſary and eternal, by Prop. XX.)
neceſſarily lays us under an Obligation to act
and behave differently towards them ; or to
conſider and treat them ſeverally, according
to their Natures, by Prop. XXII. or according to Truth, by Prop. XII. XIX. whether
Men chooſe to conſider them in this Manner
or not. Prop. VIII.

LXVI. *FAITHFULLY to treat, or
behave towards, all rational and ſenſible Beings, and the Things which may affect them,
according to their Natures, Properties, Relations, and Circumſtances, or according to the
Truth, * ſo far as known, or apprehended by*
any

---

* *TO act according to Truth*, is a right Definition of
Virtue.   But ſome have attempted to overthrow this
Definition by alleging, " That as many Truths, or true
" Propoſitions, may be affirmed of an Action morally
" wrong, as of an Action morally right : conſequent-
" ly, that an Action morally wrong, may, by this Rule,
" be as conformable to Truth, as an Action morally
" right.   For Inſtance ; it may be truly ſaid of a vir-
" tuous Action, *that it exiſts*, or is done ; *that it is
" done rightly* ; *that it is conformable to a proper Rule* ;
" *that it is beneficial, praiſe-worthy*, &c.   And it may
" alſo, on the other Hand, be as truly ſaid of a vicious
" Action ; *that it exiſts*, or is done ; *that it is wrong
" done* ; *that it is not conformable to a proper Rule* ; that
" it is *miſchievous, blameable*, &c.   Seeing, therefore,
" as many Truths, or true Propoſitions, lie on the Side
" of

any particular *Agent*, is Virtue, or *Action morally right*, Prop. VI. *and to act in a contrary Manner is* Vice, *or Action morally evil.*

A Man, who confiders himfelf as what he is in himfelf, a rational Being, attended with various Paffions, Appetites, Imperfections and Wants ; and acts agreeably to his Nature and Circumftances, by improving and ufing his Mind and Reafon for the right Direction of his Behaviour ; who manages and reftrains his Paffions and Appetites, and turns

D 2   and

" of Vice, as on the Side of Virtue, it is not only
" falfe, but ridiculous, to make *a Conformity to Truth*
" the Rule of moral Action."

ANSWER. It is granted, that fuch Truths may be affirmed of a vicious, as well as of a virtuous Action. But then fuch Truths have relation only to the ACTION ; and to the Action, after it is done and paft : but have no Relation to the OBJECT, or the Natures, &c. of Things, which are prior to the Action, and are the Rule according to which it was, or fhould have been, done. Now, when it is faid, that *Virtue is acting conformably to Truth*, the Meaning is not, that it is acting in Conformity to any Truth, that may be affirmed of the *Action* confidered as already done, or acted ; for that would be very abfurd and ridiculous : but the Meaning is, that the Action is, or fhould be done, in Conformity to the Nature, Properties and Relations of the OBJECT of Action. Which *Object*, with all the Truths belonging to it, exifted before the Action was done, and was the Rule by which it fhould be done. In fhort ; the TRUTH in the above Definition of *Virtue* hath Relation, not to the Truths belonging to the ACTION ; but to the Truths belonging to the OBJECT ; by which Truths in the Object, the Action is regulated while it is doing.

and applies them to their proper Ends and Purpofes; who guards againft his own Weakneffes and Imperfections; and is duely careful, in a juft and reafonable Way, to fupply his Wants, and provide for his own Subfiftence. The Man, who acquaints himfelt with the Relations in which he ftands to God, his Maker, from whom he has received his All, and upon whom he hath an entire Dependence; and accordingly renders unto him fincere Gratitude, Truft and Obedience. The Man who attends to the feveral Relations, in which he ftands to the Whole, or to any Part of Mankind, as a Man, a Magiftrate, a Subject, a Father, a Son, a Brother, a Hufband, a Mafter, a Servant, &c. and acts agreeably to the Truths belonging to each Relation, in Juftice, Goodnefs, Fidelity. The Man, who confiders the Sufferings and Sorrows, the Ignorance, Errors, Failings and Temptations to which Men are fubject, and treateth them with Tendernefs and Compaffion, Affiftence, Patience and Forgivenefs. Who regards any Part of the brute Creation, according to it's true Nature, as fenfible of Pleafure and Pain; as fubfervient to his Life and Interefts, and treats it accordingly, with reafonable Ufage, giving it no defigned or unneceffary Pain, fupplying it's Wants, and reafonably gratifying it's Appetites and Senfes. Laftly, who of material Things wafts and abufes nothing,

that.

that may be fubfervient to human Life: Such a one is a virtuous Perfon.

LXVII. Corol. 1. *The primary Foun-dation and Reafon of Virtue lies not in the Powers of our* Minds, *but in* Objects. For it is moft evident, that if there were no Ob-jects of right Behaviour, whatever Faculties we are endowed with, there could be no Virtue ; as there would be nothing to exer-cife thofe Faculties upon, Prop. VII. This is common to moral Philofophy with all o-ther Arts and Sciences ; whofe Ground and Foundation lies in the Objects upon which they are exercifed. Without Sounds, or Difference of Sounds, there could be no Mu-fic. Without Numbers, Dimenfions, Lines or Figures, there could be no Mathematics.

LXVIII. Corol. 2. *That Virtue and it's Obligations, being founded in Truth, or the Nature of Things, ftand upon a neceffary, eternal and immutable Foundation, not to be changed by any Will, Power, Authority, Time or Place ; but exift, and muft for ever exift independent of all thefe,* by Prop. XX, XXII.

LXIX. *ALL rational Beings, without Exception, are neceffarily and unavoidably fub-ject to the Obligations of Virtue.* For as thofe Obligations do exift neceffarily, they muft be uniformly the fame, wherever there is

Under-

Underſtanding ; or any Beings, Relations,
Properties, Circumſtances, which belong to,
or infer, any Temper of Mind, or Behavior in Actions. God therefore, who is infinite in Knowledge and Power cannot but be
obliged, in all his Actions, to act agreeably
to the *real* Natures, Relations and Circumſtances of *all* Things ; of Himſelf, and of
all other Beings, without Exception. That
is to ſay, He cannot but ſee in all Caſes,
and with Regard to all Beings, what is true,
or what is right and fit to be done ; and ſo,
is obliged by the Rule of His own infinite,
eternal and all-perfect Underſtanding, to do
what is right ; nor can He be obliged by any
Thing elſe. Nor is it poſſible He ſhould,
in any Caſe or Degree whatever, not comply
with ſuch His Obligations. For there can be
no poſſible Hindrance to His Judgment or
Actions in the leaſt Degree. The perfect
Wiſdom and Power of God, together with
His Self-ſufficiency, muſt render all His Actions, moral as well as natural, abſolutely
complete. For there can be no poſſible
Reaſon why He ſhould ever do that which is
unreaſonable, or not do that which is reaſonable ; ſeeing He neceſſarily knows what is
reaſonable, and has all Power abſolutely in
His own Hands, directed by infinitely perfect Knowledge and Wiſdom. He cannot
poſſibly want, or deſire any Thing for Himſelf ; and therefore can never poſſibly have
any

any Inducement to Action, but the *Reason of Action*. And, as it is impoffible that Reafon fhould be both for and againft any Action, it follows, that GOD will always do what is right and reafonable : not becaufe He has not the *natural* Power to do otherwife ; but becaufe He can have no Motive to it, but will always choofe to act reafonably : hence arife thofe Perfections in GOD, which are called *moral*; fuch as *Juſtice, Goodneſs, Faith-fulneſs, Truth,* and the like ; which may be comprized under the Name and Notion of *Divine Rectitude,* meaning, that Conſtancy and Certainty, with which GOD doth invariably act according to Truth and the Reafon of Things ; which is the fole Ground of his moral Perfections. And as GOD is, in the higheſt Degree, under the Obligations of Virtue ; fo all inferior rational Beings are under the fame Obligations, fo far as their Knowledge and Power can extend. And fuch Beings can never act fuitably to their rational Natures, or comply with their moral Obligations, without a conſtant and upright Exertion of all their Powers, according to their feveral Circumſtances, in the Difcovery of Truth, (fuch firſt as moſt concerns them, and fo on,) and in acting agreeably to it.

LXX. *A L L particular Obligations to act virtuouſly are included in the general one* [Prop. LXVI.] *of acting agreeably to the true Na-*

D 4

tures,

tures, &c. *of Things, and are moral Duties
only by Virtue of it's Force.* For whatever
is required of moral Agents by the Will of
God, or by the Will of any other Being;
or by the Profpect of any Happinefs, or
Freedom from Pain, can oblige them only
as *rational* Agents, or as they lie under the
Obligations of this everlafting univerfal Rule
of Action. And whatever doth not oblige
them as *rational* Agents, can be no moral
Obligation at all; but mere inftinctive Inclination, or abfurd Force and Conftraint. The
Perception of Truth being that alone, which
can poffibly render any Agent, or Action
moral. For where there is no *Truth*, or no
Truth perceived, there can be no Exercife of
Reafon, or moral Agency.

LXXI. *VIRTUE, with Refpect to it's*
Obligations, *is a Law.* And it is the FIRST
and SUPREME Law, to which all other Laws
owe their Force, on which they depend, and
in Virtue of which alone they oblige. [Prop.
LXX.] It is an UNIVERSAL Law. The
whole Creation is ruled by it: under it Men,
and all rational Beings do fubfift. [Nor is it
fit they fhould fubfift, or continue in Being,
but as they are voluntarily ruled by it.] It is
the Source and Guide of all the Actions of
DEITY Himfelf, and on it his Throne and
Government is founded. [Prop. XXIV,
LXIX.] It is an UNALTERABLE and IN-
DISPEN-

DISPENSIBLE Law. The Repeal, Sufpen-
fion, or even Relaxation of it, but for a
Moment, in any Part of the Univerfe, cannot be conceived without a Contradiction ;
[or without fuppofing Things to be what
they really are not ; or without a Diffolution
of the whole Univerfe.   It is an ETERNAL
and EVERLASTING Law.] Other Laws have
had a Date ; a Time when they were enacted and became of Force.   They are confined to particular Places, reft upon uncertain Foundations, may lofe their Vigor,
grow obfolete with Time, and become ufe-
lefs and neglected.   None of thefe are true
of this Law.   It has no Date ; was never
made or enacted ; is prior to all Things, and
governs all Things ; is felf-originated, and
felf-valid ; ftands on immoveable Foundations, and can never lofe it's Vigor and Ufe-
fulnefs ; but muft ever retain them, without the Poffibility of Diminution or Abate-
ment.   It is coeval with Eternity ; as unalterable as neceffary, everlafting Truth ; as
independent as the Exiftence of GOD ; and
as facred, venerable and awful as His Nature
and Perfections.   *Price's* Review, Chap. VI.
P. 189.

LXXII. *VIRTUE, with Refpect to the
Practice of it, is the Perfection of rational
Beings.*   Becaufe it is the only right Manner
of applying and ufing the Powers of Reafon,

in

in all Cafes and Circumftances, according to
their true Nature, and for the higheft Ends
and Purpofes for which they could be given.
For they could be given for no higher End,
than to underftand the Truth, and to act a-
greeably to it. Which muft include all good
Difpofitions of Mind ; all that can render
a moral Agent ufeful to others, and happy
in himfelf : that is to fay, all that is perfec-
tive of his Nature, both abfolutely and rela-
tively. By Virtue, one Man is a God to another. By this nobleft of all Principles we
move regularly and honorably in every Sphere
of Action ; and behave properly under all
Events in every Relation, State and Condi-
tion. And by the Habits of Virtue, gained
in this prefent World, we are duely qualified
to act *for ever* properly and worthily ; and
in a manner perfectly agreeable to any new
inlarged or exalted Circumftances, Ingage-
ments or Relations in any future State of Exiftence, and in any other Part of God's Creation, to which we can be raifed, or remov-
ed ; feeing the Laws and Obligations of Virtue are the fame every where, throughout the
whole Univerfe, and throughout all Eternity.

LXXIII. *VIRTUE is the only Mean of
rendring moral Agents the proper Objects of
Approbation, Efteem, Encouragement and Reward.* Mere Exiftence, though attended
with the higheft Powers, being fimply the
Work

Work and Gift of God, and no ways the Merit of the Agent, who poſſeſſes them, cannot recommend that Agent to Eſteem, or render him praiſe-worthy or rewardable. Moſt evidently, it is only his own proper Uſe and Application of his Being and Powers, that can give him a Character of Worth, and intitle him to Honor and Reward.

LXXIV. COROL. *It ſeems agreeable to the Reaſon of Things, that moral Agents, after their Creation, ſhould be, for ſome Time, in a State of Trial or Diſcipline* ; to exerciſe, prove and ſeaſon their Virtue in it's proper Habits, (which cannot be forced upon them. Prop. LV.) in order to render them the qualified Objects of the Divine Approbation, and the proper Subjects of Honor and Exaltation. And this may well be ſuppoſed to be the preſent Caſe of Mankind.

LXXV. *OUR Maker, by giving us rational Powers, hath neceſſarily laid us under all moral Obligations, and, conſequently, hath made us the Subjects of moral Government, as far as thoſe Powers extend,* By Prop. XL, LXIX.

LXXVI. COROL. *The promoting of Virtue among moral Agents is the End and Deſign of all the Divine Conſtitutions and Diſpenſations relating to ſuch Agents.* For God has plainly

ly declared, in the Frame of their Nature,
that he has made them for the Purpofes of
Virtue; and as this muft be the principal
End, becaufe it is the Perfection, of their
Being, [Prop. LXXII.] GOD will certainly,
and conftantly act agreeably to thefe Truths,
in all his Dealings, Appointments and Tranf-
actions with moral Agents, according as their
feveral Cafes and Circumftances do require.
[Prop. XXIV.]

LXXVII. *REASON, or Underftanding,
is the cnly Faculty in the human Conftitution,
which can perceive moral Obligations.* Becaufe
this is the only Faculty that can difcern
Truth, or the true Natures, Circumftances
and Relations of Things; [Prop. **XXXVIII.**]
and, confequently, the Obligations, which
neceffarily refult from them. [Prop. XXII.]

LXXVIII. *WITHOUT a right and
faithful Ufe of Underftanding, Virtue cannot
be practifed.* Becaufe Virtue is acting conformably to the Natures of Things; and
therefore thofe muft be known according to
our Capacity; otherwife, it is not poffible
we fhould act agreeably to them. [Prop. XV.]

LXXIX. *THEREFORE, the rational
Powers, or Intelligence, of every finite moral
Agent, is the firft, or neareft, Object of that
right Action, or virtuous Conduct, to which*
fuch

fuch Agent is obliged. [Prop. XVI.] Which mental Powers he is neceffarily obliged, or it will always be reafonable for him. to cultivate and improve, according to their Extent and Capacity, and the Opportunities he enjoys, by the general Law, which obliges him to treat or ufe every Thing according to it's true Nature. For as it is the true Nature and Ufe of the Eye to difcern Objects; and the Eye, which is always wilfully clofed, is, in Effect, deftroyed : fo it is the true Nature and Ufe of Intelligence, or Reafon, to confider and compare Objects, their Properties and Relations ; otherwife, it is, in Effect, deftroyed, and is no Underftanding, or underftands nothing as it fhould do. And fo the Conduct of the moral Agent, who neglects or perverts his Underftanding, is vicious, by the foregoing Propofition. Therefore, the primary Object of Virtue is our own Faculties, and a right Ufe of them. And the Obligation to a right Ufe of them neceffarily arifes from our being poffeffed of them. [Prop. LXXV.] That is to fay, while we are poffeffed of them, it will always be reafonable to ufe them rightly, or according to their true Nature : and can never be otherwife.   Prop. XII.

LXXX. *T H E Extent of our intellectual Capacities, and the Means and Opportunities we enjoy of improving and exerting them,*
muft

muſt be taken into the Account of our Virtue, and of the Degree of our Obligations. For Capacity, Means and Opportunity are Truths relating to our Being and Circumſtances, as much as any other whatever; and therefore, ought to be conſidered as being what they truly are. No Man can be obliged to Impoſſibilities; or it cannot be reaſonably expected, that he ſhould do no more than is in his Power. No Beings can lie under further Obligations than their Powers extend to. Prop. LXIV.

LXXXI. Corol. *The Differences of Capacities, Educations, Opportunities, and various other Circumſtances of our Exiſtence, make the Trial, or moral State, of different Men different and peculiar.* Which Difference of moral State is a Secret to our narrow Minds, and can be known to God alone.

LXXXII. GOD, *who is infinite in Power and Wiſdom, can inlarge our Faculties, diſcover new Objects of Attention and Regard; or ſupply new, and more effectual Means of Improvement, as he pleaſes.* And it is agreeable to His Character, as He is our Maker and Father, that He ſhould afford His Offspring ſuch Means of Improvement.

LXXXIII. *IF at any Time the great* GOD *hath been pleaſed, or ſhall think fit,*

to

to inlarge our Faculties, or to discover any new Object of our Regard and Attention, besides and beyond what appears to us in the present Constitution of Things ; or to supply any new or more effectual Means of improving our Minds, we are obliged, by the necessary and eternal Law of Truth, [Prop. LXVI.] *to regard and to use them according to what they are, as much as we are obliged to regard and improve those, which He hath already discovered and supplied in the present Constitution of Things.* This Rule must hold good to all Eternity. If God discovers a new Benefactor, our Gratitude immediately, and necessarily becomes due to that Benefactor. If he displays new Instances of Goodness and Favor, our Obligations to Love and Thankfulness necessarily result. If he furnishes new Motives to Duty and Virtue, we are bound by the eternal and immutable Laws of Truth, to admit their Force upon our Minds. Objects and Favors may be new ; but Obligations cannot be of a new Sort, but must be of the same Kind with any other we are at any Time under. The Sphere of Duty may be inlarged ; but Duty, or right Action must, in it's own Nature, ever remain unaltered.

LXXXIV. *A NEW, or different Relation or Circumstance, according to the eternal and immutable Law of Truth, constitutes new and different Duties, with their proper Obligations.*

gations *. When a Perfon is advanced to
Magiftracy, his Obligations and Duties, as a
Magiftrate, are different from thofe of private Life. As a private Perfon, he was
obliged indeed to be concerned for, and to
wifh well to, the whole Community; but
was not invefted with Power and Authority
to guard, or to effect it's Welfare. But as a
Magiftrate, invefted with Power and Authority to guard the Safety, and promote the
Welfare of the Whole, he is obliged by the
true Nature of the Relation, in which he
ftands to the Community, not only to wifh
it well, but to confider by what Means his
new Power is to be employed, that the Prof-
perity of the Community may be beft fecured
and promoted, and to act accordingly. As
a private Perfon he is obliged, as all private
Perfons are, by the Laws of Truth, to make
favorable Allowances for the Infirmities, Mif-
takes and Paffions of Mankind; and fo to
be of a forbearing Temper, and ready to
forgive Wrongs and Injuries. But as a Magiftrate, the State of the Community muft
determine him in difpenfing Pardons and
Punifhments, according as they affect the
State of the Public. Thus the Injury,
which

* Lines and Figures have different Properties and
Proportions, as they are differently drawn and fituated.
So the moral Qualifications of Actions vary, as their
Objects and Ends, Cafes and Circumftances alter.
[*Price.*]

which fhould always be forgiven, as it affects only a fingle Perfon, in his private Capacity, (I mean, fo far forgiven, as that he fhould not retaliate, or take a private Revenge) fhould not be forgiven by the Magiftrate, when brought before him, as it is dangerous to the Peace or Safety of the Public. And in doing Juftice, as a Magiftrate, he ought to retaliate, or proportion Punifhments to Crimes.

LXXXV. *T H E Nature of Virtue alters not with the different Capacities of Beings, only the Degree and Extent of it.* Virtue is true Virtue in *Man*, or agreeable to the Truth of Things, though infinitely inferior to, and more contracted than, Virtue in the Divine Being. The *Nature*, though not *Degree* of Virtue is the fame in all Beings. All moral Agents, fo far as their Capacities extend, are under the fame Obligations to Reafon and Truth.

LXXXVI. *T H E Foundation of moral Obligation is not affected by any Doubts or Difficulties concerning the Natures of Sub-ftances, or their Effences, no more than the Foundation of mathematical Truth.* Mathematical Truth is eternal and unalterable, whatever the Subftances of Things are, to which they relate ; and even though fuch Subftances fhould not exift at all, being

E founded

founded upon the eternal and immutable Relations and Proportions of Numbers, Lines and Figures. So moral Truth is eternal and unalterable, whether our Perceptions of Objects are true Reprefentations of their intimate Natures, or Subftances, or not. It is enough that we faithfully endeavor to perceive and underftand Objects, according to the Extent of thofe Capacities which God hath given us ; and that we act agreeably to the Ideas and Definitions of them, as they appear to the human Underftanding, whatever they are in themfelves. For we can be obliged to argue and reafon from the Natures, *&c.* of Things, and to form our Actions upon them, only as they appear to us, and are faithfully apprehended and perceived by us. Thus we fhall act agreeably to the Truth of our Capacities, and the Truth of Things, fo far as we can know them. However, in the abftract Ideas, and Definitions of Things, as they appear to us, and in their feveral Relations, Proportions and Circumftances, we cannot be deceived, unlefs we wilfully deceive our felves.

LXXXVII. *THE Imperfections, which attend our Nature, do not effect the Rule of Duty.* Seeing all Beings are neceffarily obliged to the Practice of Virtue, according to their Degree of Reafon, or moral Capacity,

city, be it more or lefs ; but no further.
For no Beings can lie under any Obligations,
beyond the Extent of their Powers or Capacities. Prop. LXXX.

LXXXVIII. *A L L the Obligations and
Duty of inferior Beings, or imperfect Agents,
are neceſſarily comprehended within the Limits
of their true and faithful Endeavors.* In
GOD, his perfect Nature excludes all Need
of Endeavors. In all imperfect Beings,
faithful Endeavors muſt be the Perfection of
their Virtue : becauſe their Powers and Capacities reach no further.

LXXXIX. *THEREFORE, in Man,
the Virtue relating to his* PRINCIPLES, *or
the Perfuaſion of his Mind concerning Duty,
cannot be meaſured either by the Quantity, or
Exactneſs of his Knowledge, or the Truth and
Rightneſs of his Opinions, but only by his real
and ſincere Love of Truth, and faithful Enquiry
after it, (according to his Capacity, Opportunities and Circumſtances,) upon which thoſe
Principles or Perfuaſions are embraced.* Becauſe this is all that he can do to gain true
Knowledge and right Opinions, how much
foever he may happen to be wrong in either.
[LXXX] His Opinions are morally right,
and have all the Merit of true ones, ſhould
they happen to be really wrong. So little
Reaſon is there for perfecuting thoſe that
really

really are ; and ftill lefs for perfecuting thofe who *we only think* are, in the Wrong.

XC. *THE Virtue relating to a Man's* Behaviour *muft be meafured by the conftant, fincere, uniform Endeavor, with which he conforms to Confcience, or the Dictates of his own Mind, according to his Powers, Affiftences and Oppofition.* The actual fincere Love of Truth is the only virtuous *Principle* in Man ; and fincere Obedience to Confcience, or the Sentiments and Perfuafions, of our Minds, is the only virtuous *Practice.* Thefe two laft Propofitions conftitute *Integrity.* It is truly and abfolutely right that a Perfon fhould do, what the Reafon of his Mind, though perhaps unhappily, but not wilfully, miftaken, requires of him : or what, according to his beft Judgment, he is perfuaded is the Will of God. If he neglects this, he becomes neceffarily and juftly the Object of his own Diflike, and forfeits all Pretenfions to Virtue and Integrity. [*Price.*]

XCI. This lays the Foundation of a Diftinction of Virtue into *abftract* and *abfolute ; practical* and *relative.* The firft denotes what an Action is in *it felf* and *abfolutely,* independently of the Senfe of the Agent, and what, if he judged truly, he would judge he ought to do. *Practical* Virtue has a neceffary Relation to, and Dependence upon, the

the Senfe and Opinion of the *Agent* concerning his Actions. It fignifies what he ought to do, upon Suppofition of his having fuch and fuch Sentiments of Things. A moral Agent may be [honeftly] miftaken ; but what in the Sincerity of his Heart he thinks he ought to do, that he ought to do, and would be juftly blameable, if he omitted to do, though contradictory to what, in the former Senfe, is his Duty, [but which he doth not fee to be his Duty.], A Magiftrate, upon the beft Evidence he can procure, may, according to his own Confcience, adjudge an Eftate to one Perfon, which according to real Right belongs to another. Not that an Action, in this Cafe, is right and wrong at the fame Time ; but it is right or wrong in different Refpects and Senfes. [*Price.*]

XCII. *TEMPTATION, or Trial, doth not leffen the general Obligation to Virtue ; though, under fome Circumftances, it may alleviate Guilt.* Cafes of extreme Danger are put ; in Reference to which it is queried, Whether we may not extricate our felves by violating the Truth, without tranfgreffing the Laws of Virtue ? The Anfwer is, By no Means. The Laws of Truth are of eternal and unalterable Obligation, by Prop. XXII, and cannot, in themfelves, and therefore ought not, in Practice, to give Way to, or to be fet afide by Hope, Shame, Fear, or

E 3 any

any other Paffion. The greateſt Loſs we can ſuſtain is that of Life. Life, by the rightful and primary Tenure, we hold, only under God and Truth ; and therefore, ſhould be willing to retain it no longer than God pleaſes; or than we can keep it without violating Truth. To loſe it in the Cauſe of Truth, is to loſe it honorably. And the Reparation of the Loſs, in that Caſe, may ſecurely be left to the Honor of the Supreme Governor. Beſides ; to ſay we may violate the Truth, in ſome Caſes of Danger, is to eſtabliſh a Rule, whereby we may be allowed to violate it, in all other Caſes of Danger ; which will open a wide Door to all Immorality, where Pleaſure and Pain, Profit and Loſs are concerned. But if Pain, Dread, Terror, or any Affection of the Mind, are ſo great as to overpower Reaſon, moral Agency, in ſuch Caſes, is deſtroyed ; nor can we be accountable for what is done or ſaid, under an Influence, which is irreſiſtible, and overbearing. But ſuch Caſes happen but ſeldom.

XCIII. *MORAL Obligations cannot, in their own Nature, interfere, or be oppoſite.* For they are all founded in Truth ; and one Truth cannot interfere with, or be contrary to, another, by Prop. XXIX. No Obligation can ſet aſide, or annul another ; but both muſt ſubſiſt together ; though imperfect

fect Beings may not be able to attend to both at once.

XCIV. *BUT there may be* Degrees *of Obligation, as there may be more Truths, or Reasons, obliging to Duty, in one Case than another.* It is true, and reasonable, that I should be kindly affected to all Men, and be ready to do any Man a good Office. But there are more Truths and Reasons obliging me, and therefore I am under greater Degrees of Obligation, to be kindly affected, and to do good Offices to those that are nearest to me in Life. But in this Case, general and particular Obligations do not interfere, so as to be opposite, or contradictory. Only as the particular Obligations require my immediate and first Attention, I may not have Power, or Opportunity, to answer the general Obligations. Which doth not ⸗prove the Nullity of those Obligations ; but the Imperfection of my Nature. They are still in Force, whenever I have Power and Opportunity to answer them ; though the Obligation be suspended, while I want Power and Opportunity, by Prop. LXXXVII. and so may be considered as not obliging at that particular Time.

XCV. *ALL Virtue is necessarily* private, *or the Result of every Person's private Judgment, and cannot be the Subject of any Autho-*

E 4 *rity*

rity whatever, any further than that Autho-
rity is judged to be reasonable, (as in martial
Affairs, or the ordering of Children,) by
Prop. XII, XXXVI. It is directly contrary
to Reason to act by the Command of another, 'till it appears to me to be reasonable
to do so. Thus my Reason and private
Judgment become the Rule, which examines
and judges the Right and Truth of Authority ; to which I am obliged to submit, not
simply because it is Authority ; but because
it is just and true Authority. But as the
great GOD can command nothing that is
wrong, by Prop. XXIV, [and therefore it is
not merely His Will, but Truth and Right
that oblige us to obey Him,] our Examina-
tion and judging of what He commands,
cannot be, as in the Case of fallible Men,
whether what He commands may not be
wrong ; but to discover the Truth and Right-
ness of what He commands ; (for so it will
certainly be found, if we judge truly ;) or
whether it be indeed His Commandment, or
not. This establishes a Right in every Man
to judge for himself.

XCVI. *VIRTUE, or moral Action, as
it is Action, can in no Sense, or Respect, be*
necessary ; *but must be necessarily and essentially free,* by Prop. XLVI. Nor can any Being be capable of it any farther than such
Being is an Agent, or is free, by Prop. LV.
XCVII.

XCVII. *BUT though Virtue is essentially the Effect of free Choice, yet the great GOD can abundantly assist our virtuous Choices and Endeavors, without interfering with our Freedom, or Agency.* As by propoſing Motives, weakning the Impreſſions of Senſe and Paſſion, throwing more Light into the Mind, comforting the Heart, ſtrengthning virtuous Deſires, Endeavors and Reſolutions.

XCVIII. *SUCH Powers as may be abuſed are eſſential to moral Agents.* Becauſe they are Agents, and, as ſuch, free to act, or not to act: to act this Way, or the contrary, by Prop. XLV, XLVI. All mere ſenſible, or animal Agents, do invariably act according to the reſpective Laws of their Natures, and obey, if not under the Conſtraint of Violence, the immediate Senſations they are under. Moral Agents can diſobey the Laws of their Natures ; and therefore ſuch Powers, as may be abuſed, are eſſential to ſuch Beings. A virtuous Perſon muſt neceſſarily have a Power of being vicious, otherwiſe, he could not be virtuous. For then he would be neceſſarily virtuous ; which is abſurd, by Prop. LV.

XCIX. *MORAL Agents are the only Beings that can reſiſt the Will of GOD.* Not the

the *abfolute* Will of God, or what *He* himfelf determines to do. To *this Will,* moral
Agents, as all other Parts of the Creation, are naturally and neceffarily fubject.
But it is the *preceptive* Will of God, which
moral Agents can refift, or His Will commanding what *they* are to do. For what He
wills them to do, or wills to be their Duty,
muft of Neceffity be in *their* Power, or fubject to their Agency; and confequently, muft
depend on them alone, with Refpect to their
Obedience. For if they cannot but obey,
or muft neceffarily obey, it *is* very plain,
they do not obey at all; but are compelled
by fome, either internal or external Force;
which deftroys the very Effence of Obedience. Prop. **LV.**

C. *VIRTUE, or Action morally right,
cannot confift in any naturally good Difpofition,
Temper or Inclination, any further than fuch
Difpofition, or Temper, is actually approved
of, and voluntarily encouraged and cultivated
in the Mind,* by Prop. **LXII.** But good
Difpofitions, which are moral Habits, or the
Effect of repeted morally good Actions, of
Attention, Care, Culture of the Mind, and
the conftant, perfevering Practice of Virtue ;
fuch good Difpofitions are virtuous. But
what is originally implanted in our Nature
cannot be our Virtue ; becaufe it cannot be
our Action.

CI. *A C-*

CI. *ACTION is essential to a virtuous Character.* No Being can be accounted good or virtuous, but only so far as it performs morally good Actions, either *internally*, in the Mind or Thoughts; or, so far as it hath Power and Opportunity, in external Practice. For a mere Capacity of Virtue, is no more Virtue, than a Capacity of Action is Action. Nor is an Intention of acting, Virtue, which Intention, when it is in the Agent's Power, is not put in Execution.

CII. *IN Morality, the End and Means are the same.** That is to say, no moral Agent should propose any End, but only so far as it is virtuous; nor pursue it by any Means, but only such as are virtuous. All other Ends are distinct from the Means of obtaining them: but in Morality both End and Means coincide, and are the same; there being no Way to Virtue, but the Practice of Virtue; nor any End to be thereby proposed, but. the Reasonableness of our Actions, and their Conformity to Truth. For to propose any other End is absurd. Because thereby the Action ceaseth to be virtuous, or reasonable, so far as that other End, which is not virtuous, or reasonable, *alone* is regarded. To propose the

---

* *Stoici dicebant, Honestatem propter se expetendam.* Cicero de Offic. Lib. I. Cap. II. Virtue is necessarily obligatory on all rational Beings, for it's own Sake alone, exclusively of what may be gained by it, or any Consequences that may flow from it. Prop. IX, X.

the greateſt Happineſs to our ſelves or others, is the moſt important End we can purſue. But to purſue this End, without perceiving or conforming to the rational Obligation ſo to do, cannot be virtuous ; but muſt only be what all mere ſenſible and animal Beings, void of any moral Capacity, and without any Perception of moral Obligation, are capable of, and conſtantly comply with, according to the Natures of their ſeveral Inſtincts, or Senſations. No Inſtance of Happineſs is to be intended, but what is reaſonable ; nor to be purſued by any Means, but ſuch as are reaſonable. If we propoſe the Favor of God or Men as an End, it muſt be purſued as a reaſonable End, by reaſonable Action, or our Conduct cannot be virtuous. For what ever is not a reaſonable Object of Purſuit cannot be purſued reaſonably, or virtuouſly. A moral Agent is bound to purſue Happineſs, Honor or Glory : but in no other Way than what is ſuitable to the Nature of Things ; that is to ſay, by acting in Conformity to the true Nature of the Object, his own Nature, and all other Circumſtances. Therefore the *mere* Purſuit of Happineſs is not Virtue ; but the purſuing it *reaſonably* is Virtue. Therefore, even in ſeeking Happineſs, the End is ſtill being virtuous, or approving our ſelves to our own Minds, as having done Right in the purſuit of Happineſs ; not merely as having gained Happineſs or Enjoyment, but as having gained it as a reaſonable

able

able and virtuous End, by reasonable and virtuous Means. A Brute might applaud it self as having gained what is pleasing to it's Appetite. The being simply pleased with any Degree of Enjoyment, hath, in it self, no Connection with Virtue, or right moral Action ; the proper Pleasure of Virtue reaching no farther than being satisfied or pleased in having acted virtuously. Any other Pleasure must be of the same Kind with animal Pleasures, *viz.* only the Perception, or Feeling, of some Sense. Vicious Persons pursue Happiness, Pleasure or Enjoyment, as well as the virtuous. Therefore, with the mere Pursuit of Enjoyment, neither Virtue nor Vice are in any Connection, being a mere natural, instinctive Object or Pursuit. The Difference is, the virtuous do not make Pleasure or Happiness the primary and principal End of their Pursuit, but the being virtuous, or acting virtuously : the vicious make Pleasure and Happiness the primary and principal End of their Pursuit, without any Regard to being virtuous.

CIII. *T H O S E Actions are indifferent, with Respect to which there is no Room for the Exercise of Reason, or a Regard to Truth ;* if any such Actions can be. But no Action can be indifferent, where there is any Place for the Exercise of Reason.

CIV. *A S*

CIV. *AS the Circumstances of Actions are very different, and their Degrees of Importance are infinite ; so the moral Obligations in many Actions are very small and few.*

CV. *ALL merely animal, material and insensible Things can reasonably be regarded in our Actions, only according to their Uses and proper Applications to rational and sensible Beings.* To this Rule muſt be reduced the extirpating of Weeds, the pruning, and felling of Trees, the deſtroying of noxious Creatures, and the taking away the Lives of others for Food ; which is indeed contrary to their ſeveral Natures, conſidered ſimply as living and growing ; but agreeable to their Natures, or to the Truth, as they are either hurtful, or ſubſervient to human Life. For as they are not capable of uſing themſelves, or of directing their Being, or Faculties, to rational Ends, they are to be uſed and directed by rational Agents according to their Natures, and Capacities of Uſefulneſs, or of the contrary.

CVI. *IT is immoral and contrary to the true Natures of the Things, to deſtroy without Reaſon, any material Things, that may be uſeful to rational or ſenſible Beings.*

CVII. *IT*

CVII. *IT is immoral unneceffarily to take away Life from, or to give unneceffary Pain to, any fenfible Being whatever.*

CHAP. VI.

Of Happiness.

CVIII. DEFIN. *HAPPINESS is agreeable Senfations, or pleafant Feelings of Mind, or Body, in a Freedom from all that may give Uneafinefs.* Happinefs may otherwife be called *Pleafure* or *Enjoyment* ; and the Means of producing or obtaining Happinefs, may be called *Good, Profit, Advantage, Intereft.*

CIX. *BY the Definition Happinefs is effentially different from Virtue.* For,

CX. 1. *Happinefs is a pleafing Senfation ; Virtue is right Action.* But to feel what is pleafant, and to do what is right, are in Nature quite diftinct. Mere Animals can perceive Happinefs, or pleafing Senfations, and are capable of purfuing them, without being able at all to diftinguifh or practife moral Good or Evil. And therefore, a Senfe or Capacity of Happinefs is not neceffarily connected

nected with, much lefs can it conftitute, moral Agency.

CXI. 2. *HAPPINESS is a Manner or State of Exiflence ; Virtue is a Manner of Action.* Every Manner or State of Exiftence is the Effect of Power not our own, producing it independently of our Choice ; as whether we fhall be in Health or Sicknefs, in Peace or Trouble, in a chearful Temper or in low Spirits, and fad Dejection of Mind. But Virtue is the Choice of our own Wills, and is always abfolutely in our own Power. We cannot at all alter the State and Manner of our Being, as originally conftituted : nor can we always, and perhaps but in few Inftances, alter the State and Manner of our Being, as it may afterwards accidentally be attended with Pain and Suffering. But whatever is the Manner and State of our Being, we can always be virtuous.

CXII. 3. *HAPPINESS is the Gift, Operation, Conflitution or Appointment of GOD alone, and can be neither more nor lefs, than what he willeth, or effecteth ; whether it arifeth from the proper Exercife of thofe Powers he hath given to any Being, or be referved to his wife and equitable Diflribution in fome future Time.* For the Divine Power is abfolute over all Beings, Minds and Bodies without Exception. And as he can

put

put them into any State or Mode of Being as
he pleafeth ; fo it is not poffible they fhould,
either by their own Actions, or otherwife,
be in any State of Being, but what he effects
or hath conftituted. For as no Creature can
give it felf Exiftence ; fo neither can it give
it felf any particular State of Exiftence ; but
muft neceffarily take it's Exiftence, as capable of Pleafure, or obnoxious to Pain,
juft as God hath allotted, and appointed ;
who, if he had pleafed, could have made
thofe Objects or Actions the Occafion of the
greateft Pleafure, which are now the Occafion of the greateft Pain or Uneafinefs. But
Virtue is the Act and Choice of our own
Mind, independent of the Will and Pleafure
of God ; who cannot alter it's Nature, or
change a virtuous Action into it's contrary ;
as he can turn the Senfations, which are now
pleafurable, into fuch as are painful, and *vice
verfâ*.

CXIII. 4. *NO Being can be happy without a Power, Force or Strength, fufficient to
fecure to it felf whatever is agreeable and
pleafing to it's Nature, and renders it's Cir-
cumflances perfectly eafy on the one Hand ; and
on the other to guard and preferve itfelf in
perfect Safety from all Annoyance, or from
whatever may occafion Pain, Sorrow, Solici-
tude and Dejection of Mind.* Happinefs, or
pleafing Senfations of Body or Mind, is ne-

ceffarily

ceffarily the Effect of *Power*, and fubject to
it. But rational Beings may be virtuous in
fole *Agency*, or in a Capacity of choofing to
do what is *right*.

CXIV. 5. *SUFFERING and Sorrow,
the Oppofites to Happinefs, may be the moft
proper Means of gaining the higheft Degree of
Happinefs : but Falfhood and Vice, the Oppofites of Virtue, can in no Inftance, or Refpect,
be any Means of gaining Virtue, or of rendring
thofe, who practife them, virtuous.*

CXV. 6. *MORAL Obligations and Happinefs may interfere ; but moral Obligations
never do, nor can, interfere with each other.*
Prop. XV. XCIII. Nothing is more common
than for the Practice of Virtue to be attended
with Suffering in one Kind or other.

CXVI. 7. *HAPPINESS is of a va-
rious, uncertain Nature ; and depends upon the
Apprehenfions, Opinions, Tempers, Difpofitions,
and even Imaginations of Men.* He is not
happy, who doth not think himfelf fo ; or,
who is not in a Temper for relifhing what
otherwife would give Happinefs or Enjoyment. But Virtue is of a certain and unalterable Nature, and has no Dependence
upon Temper, Conceit or Opinion.

CXVII.

CXVII. V_IRTUE_ *therefore and* Happinefs *are in their feveral* Natures *effentially different and diflinct*; quite unconnected and independent, as much as Senfation or Feeling, the Effect of mere Power or Force, is diftinct from, and unconnected with, right Action, or the free Choice of a moral Agent; or as much as a good Character is different from, and unconnected with, the enjoying of a good Eftate, or the relifhing of pleafant Food.

CXVIII. *HAPPINESS, or the Enjoyment of Good, cannot be the proper Foundation, primary Reafon, or catholic Rule of Virtue; though, in a rational Way, it may be a Motive to it.* It cannot be the primary Reafon, or Rule of Virtue; becaufe Virtue is, in it's own Nature, diftinct, and may exift feparate from Happinefs, and confequently, may be where Happinefs is not. Our Senfations may be fometimes agreeable, fometimes difagreeable : but under all fuch Changes, the Obligations of Virtue are not affected, but remain unalterably the fame, ftanding upon an eternal and immutable Bafis. Further ; Happinefs, Enjoyment or Good, cannot be the abfolute and univerfal Rule of Duty; becaufe thefe are not *always*, and *in every Inftance*, a proper Rule of Duty, or Object of Purfuit. For the Rule of Duty in many Cafes will lead us to Suffering, and oblige

F 2   us

us to refufe and pay no Regard to Enjoyment, Advantage, Good or Happinefs. But that Rule, which is not *univerfal*, at all Times and in all Cafes the fame, cannot be the Foundation of Virtue : becaufe fuch a Rule would be uncertain and various ; and fo, fometimes it's contrary would be the Rule. But Truth is immutable, always, and in all Cafes, the invariable Rule of Conduct. Prop. XX, LXVIII. Therefore, the Truth is the only proper Foundation of Virtue.

CXIX. HAPPINESS *is not the* neceffary *Confequence of Virtue.* Becaufe, in many Cafes, Suffering attends Virtue, or is the Confequence of it. But *Neceffity* is a Principle, cr Reafon, which fubfifts equally, and univerfally, at all Times, every where, and in all Cafes. Therefore, if Happinefs were *neceffarily* connected with Virtue, the virtuous could not but be *always* actually happy, and every where, and in all Cafes, poffefs Enjoyment, in Proportion to the Degree of their Virtue. But this is contrary to certain Fact and Experience ; which is Evidence as clear and ftrong as the moft certian Experiment in natural Philofophy, and abfolutely overthrows the Notion, that Happinefs is the *neceffary* Confequence of Virtue. For, if but one fingle rightlin'd Triangle could at any Time be found, in any Part of the Univerfe, whofe

three

three Angles added together could be de-
monſtrated to be more or leſs than two Right-
Angles, that ſingle Inſtance would overthrow
the *neceſſary* and *univerſal* Truth of this Propoſition, *That in every rightlin'd Triangle the
three Angles taken together are equal to two
Right-Angles.* In like Manner, if there can
be found but one Inſtance, (and many In-
ſtances may be found) of diſtreſſed, ſuffer-
ing Virtue, it muſt abſolutely deſtroy the
Truth of this Propoſition, *That Happineſs is
the* neceſſary *Conſequence of Virtue.* The
moſt virtuous Perſons may be in Pain,
Trouble, Sorrow, and ſad unaccountable Dejection of Spirit and Horror of Mind. Nor
can their Virtue free them from their Sufferings. This can be done only by ſome
Power, Force or Strength, by Prop. CXIII.
But Virtue, (eſpecially conſidered as already
performed or practiſed,) is not Power,
Force or Strength. Virtue is Action, but
not an Agent ; and it's Action, as ſuch, ter-
minates wholly in it ſelf, or is it's own End.
The proper End of Virtue, or right Action,
being to act rightly, to regulate our Behavior,
or to conſtitute a virtuous Character. Virtue,
in it ſelf, extends no further, by Prop. CII.
Virtue, indeed, in any Caſes of Diſtreſs,
where it is remembered and attended unto,
(for it may poſſibly be forgot, or not attended
unto, and then certainly it can give no Re-
lief) will ſupply comfortable, alleviating
Conſiderations. But in ſuch Caſes, when it

is

is remembered and attended unto, the only Reflection, relating to Virtue, is, that we have acted virtuously, that we have done no Wrong. All the reft, even all the Comfort, is an Inference from this; *namely*, therefore we have not deferved thofe Sufferings : or therefore fome juft Power will interpofe to deliver us from them. Confolation is not the immediate Effect of Virtue, which is no Caufe, no Agent, but the Inference of our Minds drawn from the Virtue to which we are confcious ; which Inference may, or, through Excefs of Anguifh, may not, be made : if not, then no Confolation will follow from Virtue. Thus a Perfon under a painful Diforder, if he reflects, may have fome Comfort, from this Confideration, that *it cannot hold long.* Now, it is not the Diftemper, in it felf, that effects this Comfort; but the Reflection or Inference of the Mind, that it muft foon be over. Virtue, when we have practifed it, is no Power, no Agent, but only a Notion, or abftract Idea, in our Minds, which can effect nothing, but as it is remembered, reflected upon, and Inferences are drawn from it. Indeed *We*, ourfelves, are Agents, and have Power ; but not Power to make ourfelves or others happy, by guarding againft all poffible Evils, or fecuring the Poffeffion and Enjoyment of *all*, or any Good fuitable to our Nature in this World ; much lefs, in a future State. God only hath Power to do this.

CXX. *BUT*

CXX. *BUT though Virtue is not the* neceſſary Cauſe *of Happineſs, yet it is* neceſſarily *the only Ground of Happineſs* ; as it is
true, that Virtue is the higheſt Perfection of
rational Nature, which is the moſt excellent
Kind of Being ; [LXXII.] and as Virtue is
the only Object of Reward, Encouragement,
Protection and Honor. [LXXIII.] This re-
ſults from the intrinſic Excellence of Virtue,
as it is right Action. And this muſt lay an
Obligation upon, or make it fit and reaſonable for, the great GOD, who alone hath
Power to confer Happineſs, to make Virtue
finally happy. Though, (as he muſt be
obliged to give Happineſs in a rational Way,)
He may have preponderating Reaſons for a
while, or in a State of Trial, to ſuſpend
Happineſs, or to permit the Sufferings even
of virtuous Beings ; as, if for no other
Reaſon, to prove, exerciſe and raiſe their
Virtue, to it's proper Degree of Strength and
habitual Perfection. To this Obligation we
are ſure GOD, the moſt perfect Intelligence, doth, in every State of Things, conſtantly and invariably attend ; and therefore
we are as ſure, that the virtuous will be
happy, as we are of the Effects of any of
the divine moral Perfections. And even in
the preſent State of Things, GOD hath ſup-
plied us with Facts and Experience ſuffi-

cient

cient to shew, that Virtue will be finally happy.*

CXXI. Corol. 1. *There can be no other Way of being happy, but in the Practice of Virtue.* Because we can in no other Way attain to the Perfection of our Nature, procure Satisfaction, Peace and Comfort of Mind, or gain the Favor of God. Happiness is *neceffarily* connected with no Power we have, and cannot be procured without the Will of God ; therefore the Practice of Virtue, which muft be his Will, is the only Way, and the infallible Way, to obtain it.

CXXII. Corol. 2. *The Scriptures are true in directing us to a Dependence upon GOD alone, and to feek unto him for Happiness ; for Success, Safety, Peace, and a comfortable Enjoyment of ourfelves, in an abfolute Truft in his Goodness, Submiffion to his Will, and in the Ufe of fuch Means only as he hath appointed*
for

* THE Obligation to the Practice of Virtue, in a State of Things, where it frequently expofes the Virtuous to Suffering and Mifery, would be an abfurd Conftitution, if there was not a moral Governor of the World, upon whom virtuous Beings might depend for final Happinefs, in the Practice of Virtue. For either all virtuous Beings fhould be infenfible to Pleafure and Pain ; or Pleafure fhould always, in all Circumftances, attend Virtue, neither of which is true in Fact ; or elfe, (which is the Truth,) there muft be a moral Governor of the Univerfe. *Enquiry concerning Virtue,* &c.

for promoting our preſent or future well-being.

CXXIII. Corol. 3. *Happineſs, or Self-Enjoyment, is the* * *natural Effect of Virtue*; that is to ſay, by the Will and Conſtitution of God : even as Light is the natural Effect of the Sun, or Nouriſhment the natural Effect of eating. The Sun, by the general Conſtitution of it's Nature, would ſhine upon us always, did not God appoint Clouds, and the Interpoſition of the Earth, to intercept it's Rays : and Food would always nouriſh the Body, had not God, in certain Caſes, and for wiſe Ends, ordained, that Diſeaſes ſhould interrupt it's natural Efficacy, even when it is uſed according to the ſtricteſt Rules of Temperance. So Virtue would naturally, that is, by the general Conſtitution of God, produce pleaſing, and Vice diſpleaſing Senſations, unleſs God is pleaſed by his Power to interpoſe in either Caſe. For the human Mind, as all dependent Beings, is neceſſarily ſubject to the abſolute Power of God. He can make what Impreſſions He pleaſes upon our Spirits, to depreſs or to raiſe them, to ſuſpend their Powers or Reflections, to abate their Vigor, and, in ſhort, totally to anni-
hilate

---

* In this, and the next Propoſition, I uſe the Word *natural*, in Oppoſition to *neceſſary* : meaning thereby, the mere Will of God, or what he has been pleaſed to appoint.

hilate them. The Mind cannot poſſibly be in any State of Pleaſure or Uneaſineſs, but what God is pleaſed to effect, conſtitute or permit. Thus the very beſt of Men may, unaccountably, be under very ſad Dejections of Mind, without the leaſt Comfort from their Integrity ; while vicious Perſons may be jovial and merry, without any preſent Interruption from a Senſe of Guilt. Both which Caſes muſt be by the Permiſſion of God, or his Impreſſions upon the Mind ; and both in much Wiſdom adapted to a State of Trial, where the Virtue of good Men is to be variouſly exerciſed ; and where, if the natural Conſequences of Vice were always to take Place, bad Men would not be free, but forced to be virtuous : which is a Contradiction, by Prop. XCVI, LV.

By the Way, I cannot ſee how Beings, that have contracted Guilt, perhaps in a heinous Degree, can, though pardoned, be happy in a future State, unleſs the Divine Power, by it's Impreſſions, ſuſpends or ſuppreſſes Reflections upon their Guilt, or takes off the Force of Truth, by taking off the Attention of their Minds to it. Otherwiſe, were they always attentive to it, the Truth relating to every Inſtance and Degree of Guilt would be the ſame, and their Senſe of it the ſame to all Eternity, by Prop. XXVII. No Truth can be deſtroyed ; but the Attention and

and Affections of the Mind may be altered, by the Impreffions of Almighty Power.

CXXIV. *T H E Happinefs or Pleafures, which naturally attend the Practice of Virtue, are the greateft we are capable of enjoying in this imperfect State.* Becaufe they are the Refult of the righteft and beft Ufe of our nobleft Powers. Which Ufe of our Powers, when the free and juft Exercife of them is not hindered, clouded or fufpended, by mental Diforders, exceffive Pains, or everwhelming Sorrows, muft, therefore, when reflected upon, yield a Pleafure, Satisfaction or Comfort, in the Confcioufnefs of our Integrity, the inward Approbation of our own Actions; and a Senfe of the Divine Favor, as much fuperior to any other Pleafure we are capable of, as the Mind, and it's Perceptions, is fuperior to the Body, and the Senfations thereof. Without this Pleafure, a Man may be in Mifery, with all other Ingredients of Happinefs; and with it, the meaneft Circumftances are not only comfortable, but infinitely preferable to all the criminal Enjoyments of Affluence.

CXXV. *HAPPINESS, as all other Ends, is only to be purfued, when it is reafonable, or, in Confiftence with, all other Truth and Obligation.* For Truth and Obligation are not alterable by any Circumftances or Profpects

pects of Pleafure and Pain, by Prop. XX, XXII. Where Truth and Reafon require certain Actions, no Intereft of Pleafure or Pain can alter the Obligation ; fince in that Cafe, a lefs Pleafure, or even Pain, is to be chofen, not indeed for it's own Sake, which is abfurd, but for the Sake of Virtue, Reafon or Truth, which moral and rational Beings are obliged to obferve. Therefore,

CXXVI. *HAPPINESS is only an End fubordinate to Truth and Reafon.* By moral Agents, or reafonable Beings, not Pleafure or Pain, but Reafonablenefs, the acting reafonably,, or according to the Obligations of Truth, is, in the Nature of Things, firft to be confidered, and is therefore the final End, by Prop. CII. And after *that*, the Confideration of any other End, and of Happinefs, in particular, may take Place ; which, therefore, can only be a fubordinate End. He acts againft Reafon, who doth not make it his firft and principal Intention and Aim to act reafonably. This is the general Law of his Nature, and ought to be the primary View and End of all his Actions.

CXXVII. *HAPPINESS, as the fole End of Action, can never be purfued reafonably, or according to Truth, except when Happinefs alone conflitutes the Obligation to purfue it.* For if there is in any Cafe, any other
Obligation

Obligation different from Happiness, or inconfiftent with it, fuch Obligation is negative
to the Purfuit of Happinefs, or forbids the
Purfuit of it. Becaufe it muft then be inconfiftent with fome Reafon or Truth ; that
is, it muft be unreafonable to purfue it. For
Happinefs is not reafonable, but when it hath
all Reafon and Truth on it's Side, or not
againft it. All Happinefs, or Pleafure, of
any Kind, muft neceffarily give Way to
Reafon; and no more is to be endeavored
after, than is confiftent with Duty. Therefore, Happinefs can never be the Objeĉt of
any moral Confideration, but when Aĉtions
relate to that alone.

CXXVIII. *HAPPINESS is a proper
Motive to Virtue.* Or, *to praĉtife Virtue in
Hopes of either prefent Comfort, or future
Happinefs, is to praĉtife it with Regard to it's
natural Confequence* ; [Prop. CXXIII.] and
therefore is perfeĉtly confiftent with the Love
of Truth, and with the true Nature of Virtue.
Or thus ; *to purfue Happinefs by the Praĉtice
of Virtue, is to purfue it in the only right,
juftifiable, and effeĉtual Method.* Becaufe then
we purfue Happinefs in Subordination to every
moral Obligation ; [Prop. CXXV, CXXVI.]
or we expeĉt Happinefs as the Reward of
nothing but Virtue; and as the Gift of GOD,
who can love and favor us, only fo far as we
are virtuous. It is recommending our felves

to

to the Approbation and Efteem of the moft
pure and perfect moral Agent, by being virtuous as he is virtuous ; who, for that Reafon, will infallibly make us finally happy.
[Prop. CXX.] Indeed, fo far as Happinefs ·
alone is regarded, and fo far as we are determined to purfue it, in any Way, right or
wrong, our Regard to Happinefs is vicious.
But to choofe, and refolve to purfue it in no
other Way than what is quite honorable, that
is to fay, in the Practice of Virtue and Truth,
and to refufe it in any other Way, is to act
in Confiftence with the moft perfect Kind,
and higheft Degree of Virtue.

CXXIX. *HAPPINESS, Pleafure, Enjoyment, are, in their own Nature, preferable
to Mifery, Pain and Suffering.* And therefore, where no other moral Obligation interferes, lay every Perfon under a moral Obli- ·
gation to purfue the one, and avoid the other,
by all Means in his Power. Becaufe thus
he acts according to their true Nature, and
the Truth of his own Nature, which requires it of him. To act otherwife, would
be to mifbehave towards himfelf, or to treat
himfelf differently from what he is, and to
neglect one of the moft important Concern-
ments of Life.

CXXX. For the fame Reafon, *it is our
Duty, when no other Obligation interferes, to*
                                    make

make all other Beings happy, as far as our Power extends, and as far as they ſtand in Need of our Aſſiſtence. That is to ſay, it is our Duty to make others happy, as far as it is reaſonable ; or ſo far as Things and Circumſtances do in Reaſon and Truth require. Otherwiſe, we ſhall miſbehave towards them, by treating them differently from what their Nature, Relations to us, and Circumſtances really are. Not to ſay, that by refuſing our good Offices, we ſhall preclude our ſelves from all Right to their Aſſiſtence, when we ſtand in Need of it. The Deſire and Study to promote univerſal Happineſs, or public Good, ſeems to be the moſt excellent Kind of Virtue, as it is the moſt conſpicuous and comprehenſive.

. CXXXI. *T H E Happineſs of the whole Univerſe, or of any Part of it, is not a reaſonable End merely for it's own Sake, and in all Circumſtances, without any Regard to the Reaſonableneſs of it.* For then it would be impoſſible to ſee any Inſtance of Pain, Suffering or Miſery, in the Univerſe, or in any Part of it, conſidering the infinite Power, Wiſdom and Goodneſs of God ; who muſt ſee the Reaſonableneſs of the ſuppoſed univerſal Happineſs, muſt be diſpoſed to will it, and who cannot poſſibly want Power in any Inſtance to effect it. Which demonſtrates, that it is not always right and reaſonable to give Pleaſure ;
but

but that our own Happinefs, and that of others is to be endeavored and promoted, only fo far as it is reafonable, or agreeable to Truth. Prop. CXXVI.

CXXXII. *IN Cafes, where it is reafon-able to purfue Happinefs, it is always reafon-able to choofe the greateft; and of Pains the leaft.*

C H A P.   VII.

Of the Will of G O D.

CXXXIII. *T*HE *Will of G O D is necef-farily under the Obligations of Truth and Right*; and is as much more cer-tainly and immutably determined by them, than the Will of any inferior rational Being, as He is infinitely more perfect than any of his Creatures. For, obferve, His Obligation to do right, is the Refult of His own infinite, eternal, and all-perfect Underftanding, and of nothing befides. [Prop. XXIV.]

CXXXIV. Corol. *G O D cannot alter any eternal and neceffary Obligations that moral Agents lie under*; fince thofe do equally, or, in Proportion to His infinite Perfection, more ftrongly, bind God Himfelf. But in all other Cafes, He may difpofe of His own,
that

that is to fay, of the whole Univerfe, and all the Being, Life, Power and Property in it, in what Manner He pleafes, without any Wrong to his Creatures ; for He is abfolute Proprietor of all.

CXXXV. *H E that aƌeth according to Truth, or the true Natures of Things, to the beſt of his Knowledge, muſt aƌ agreeably to the Will of G O D, and cannot but be approved by Him.* Obedience to Truth and Reafon, is Obedience to God.* The Laws of our Nature are the fureſt Indication of the Will of God.

CXXXVI. *I N Virtue, of the general and eternal Law of Truth, the Will of G O D is of the higheſt Authority, and abſolutely indiſputable.* For He is infinitely excellent, the fole Fountain of Reafon and Wifdom, our Maker and Proprietor, from whom we have received our ALL, and upon whom we entirely depend ; † for whom, therefore, we

---

* Λοη ω ερθω πειθεϚκι και Θεω ταυτον εϚι. *Hieroc. Carm. Pythag.*

† It is thefe render him the proper Objeƈt of our eternal Homage, conſtitute his Right of Government, veſt him with univerfal and juſt Dominion, and make it the fupreme Duty of all reafonable Beings to obey, pleafe and honor him, in all they think or do : [*Price.*] for his Nature, and Relations to them, make this their moſt reafonable Duty.

G   ought

ought to have the higheſt Eſteem and Regard, and to whoſe Commands we are bound
to yield the moſt implicit Obedience ; as we
know that the divine Will is always under
the Direction of the moſt perfect Reaſon; and
therefore is always moſt perfectly wiſe, good
and righteous. But the Will, or Command
of GOD, can poſſibly lay no moral Obligation on a rational Being, contrary to, or ſeparate from, this firſt, great and immutable
Law, any more than the Nature of Truth,
or the eternal Differences of Things, or the
Rule of everlaſting Righteouſneſs, can be
altered by the Will of GOD ; who, indeed,
hath no Will to alter them.

CXXXVII. *G O D cannot but be the
Judge of all moral Actions and Agents.* Seeing he cannot but know all Beings, and Actions, in all their Natures and Circumſtances ;
and cannot but approve or diſlike their Actions, according to the true Natures and Circumſtances of them.

CXXXVIII. *IT, is very fit and becoming
the univerſal moral Judge, to interpoſe in our
World, and to declare poſitively, as he ſhall
judge expedient, his* preſent *Approbation of
Virtue, and Diſlike of Vice* ; *and his Reſolu-
tion finally to reward the one, and to puniſh the
other.* For as he neceſſarily judgeth, and
approveth or condemneth, all moral Agents,
according

according to their Behavior, and yet, doth
not, at prefent, think proper to interpofe in
every State of their Exiftence, in order to
fhew (by apparent Difplays of his Power
rewarding and punifhing) this his Approbation or Diflike, which might be inconfiftent
with our Circumftances, as we are now in
a State of Probation. And as this Favor and
Difpleafure of God are moft of all obfcure,
(though ever certain in the Judgment of right
Reafon,) in the Imperfection and Corruption
of any State ; and as our State is manifeftly
very imperfect and corrupt, and the vifible
Diftinction between the Virtuous and Vicious
in it is very fmall, and generally not difcerni-
ble. Add to this, the Darknefs and Diffi-
culty that muft needs attend fo imperfect and
corrupt a State, and the Difcouragement and
Fear, perhaps Defpair, that muft often affect
the Hearts of weak and frail Beings, in fuch
a State ; efpecially under a Senfe of Guilt,
(and who can fay he is free ?) and the Confideration of the kind Regards and Goodwill
of God, to all his Creatures ; and it will
not be incredible, but highly probable, that
the great Governor and Judge of the World
fhould fupply thefe Defects, and fupport fuch
Beings, by fome REVELED pofitive Affurance
of his Regard and Favor, Anger and juft
Difpleafure, according to the Behavior of his
Creatures.

G 2   CXXXIX.

CXXXIX. REVELATION *cannot contra-dict, much leſs annul, the Obligations of* Natural Religion, by Prop. XXIII, XXVII. Revelation may lay new Obligations, by Prop. LXXXIII. but only in perfect Agreement with the eternal Laws of Truth, which can never be vacated.

CXL. *THE greateſt Evidence of the Truth of any* Revelation, *muſt be it's Agreement with natural Religion, or with our moral Obligations, and it's Suitableneſs to the true Circumſtances of our State.* For ſo it cannot be wrong, but muſt be right in it ſelf. Nothing can be more certainly the Will of GOD, than what Reaſon requires : and no Revelation can be more worthy of GOD, than ſuch a one as the true State of Things requires.

C H A P. VIII.

Of the human Conſtitution, with Reſpect to Morality.

CXLI. *MAN hath ſeveral other Powers beſides Reaſon and Agency.* Namely, ſundry Inſtincts, Paſſions, Affections and Appetites.

CXLII. *ALL*

CXLII. *ALL Inſtinɛts and Paſſions in our Conſtitution are inferior to Reaſon, and ſubjeɛt to it's Dominion,* by Prop. XXXIX.

CXLIII. *INSTINCTS and Paſſions are implanted in our Nature for wiſe and good Purpoſes.* This is ſufficiently aſcertained by the Wiſdom and Goodneſs of God.

CXLIV. *SOME of them are Auxiliaries to Reaſon, to excite it to Aɛtion ; and ſo are ſubſervient to the Purpoſes of Virtue.*

CXLV. *THE Paſſions are to be moderated and direɛted, as the Natures and Degrees of them, and the Circumſtances of Things do require.*

CXLVI. *CONSCIENCE is not a diſtinɛt Faculty in the human Soul; but the Judgment of our Minds concerning our own Actions ; or it is our Apprehenſions of Right and Wrong, either direɛting, or refleɛting upon, our own Conduɛt.* It differs from Reaſon and Underſtanding no otherwiſe, than as it is Reaſon or Underſtanding, exerciſed in forming a Judgment upon our own Actions, as morally right or wrong, according to that Knowledge and Conceptions of Things, which we have attained.

CXLVII.

CXLVII. *CONSCIENCE leads us according to the Judgment we form of Things.*

CXLVIII. *IN order to our being rightly directed by Conscience, it is our Duty sincerely, diligently and impartially, laying aside all Prejudice, and guarding against all Deception, to make faithful Enquiry after the Truth, and to gain the clearest Knowledge of it we are able,* by Prop. XV, XVI, LXXIX.

CXLIX. *THUS endeavouring to gain the clearest Knowledge of Truth and Right, we are obliged to perform those Actions, which our Conscience, or Judgment, apprehends to be our Duty in any Case or Circumstance.* For thus we answer the peculiar Obligations, to which we are subject, in a sincere Use of our own Capacities, Opportunities, Means and Advantages, whether they afford us more or less Light, by Prop. LXXXVII, LXXXVIII. It is all we have, and all we can have at present.

F I N I S.